Solemates

and other stories

Scottish Arts Trust Story Awards
Volume Five
2023

Edited by
Sara Cameron McBean
and Claire Rocha

Scottish Arts Trust

Praise from Ian Rankin

On *The Many Coffees of Marissa* by Kate Segriff

> *This is so clever and fresh in its approach... I hadn't seen anything like it before.*

On *Hot Wind* by Mandy Wheeler

> *...a bequest from a deceased tyrant of a father... quickly turns into a compelling mystery and a moving story of hidden lives and past indiscretions. A very elegant structure which goes beyond the narrow parameters of the whodunit.*

On *The Clear Out* by Patrick McLoughney

> *...rich in descriptive language, a deeply moving examination of a life.*

Praise from Zoë Strachan and Louise Welsh

On *The All Of It, It Misses You, Come Home*
by Sheena Cook Kopman

> *...a story for our time that is also timeless... almost every line carries a beautiful image that sings to you...*

On *Life Goes On* by Jonathan Sellars

> *delightfully irreverent... loved the voice...*

On *Join Hands* by Sean Gill

> *Terrific story with a great filmic quality... about love, endurance, bravery... made me cry.*

Other publications from the Scottish Arts Trust

The Desperation Game and other stories from the Scottish Arts Trust Story Awards 2014-2018 (Volume 1). Edited by Sara Cameron McBean and Hilary Munro (2019)

Life on the Margins and other stories from the Scottish Arts Trust Story Awards 2019-2020 (Volume 2). Edited by Sara Cameron McBean and Michael Hamish Glen (2020)

A Meal for the Man in Tails and other stories from the Scottish Arts Club Story Awards 2021 (Volume 3). Edited by Sara Cameron McBean and Michael Hamish Glen (2021)

Beached and other stories from the Scottish Arts Club Story Awards 2022 (Volume 4). Edited by Sara Cameron McBean and Claire Rocha (2022)

Rosalka: The Silkie Woman and other stories, plays and poems by Isobel Lodge (2018)

Writing Awards at the Scottish Arts Trust

Enter our writing competitions through our website at
www.scottishartstrust.org

Short Stories

First prize £3,000: The Scottish Arts Club Short Story
Competition is open to writers worldwide and stories on any
topic up to 2,000 words. Enter from 1 December to 28 February.

First prize £750: The Isobel Lodge Award is for the top short
story entered in the competition by an unpublished writer living
in Scotland.

First Prize: £300: The Write Mango Award – for the top short
story that is fun, amusing, bizarre and as delicious as a mango!

Flash Fiction

First prize £2,000: The Edinburgh Award for Flash Fiction is
open to writers worldwide and stories on any topic up to 250
words. Enter from 1 June to 31 August.

First Prize £500: The Golden Hare Award is for the top flash
fiction entry by a writer living in Scotland, published or
unpublished.

First Prize: £300: The Write Mango Flash Award – for the top
flash fiction story that is fun, amusing, bizarre and as delicious
as a mango!

Authors of at least 20 leading entries from the short story and
flash fiction competitions are offered publication in our next
anthology.

Contents

The Many Coffees of Marissa
by Kate Segriff

Winner, Edinburgh Short Story Award 2023

When things get too intense for Marissa, she buys herself a Cocoa Cluster Frappucchino, leans against the outside wall of her office building, and tells herself to breathe. When her heart rate returns to normal, she tips back her cup, reads whatever mash-up of her name the baristas have written on its side, and for eight sweet minutes she closes her eyes, and becomes that person.

"MYLISSA"

Mylissa is a ripped lioness with her jaw firmly clenched around the throat of corporate America. She had a great idea for the new lip-balm campaign today and at the 'Strategy Huddle' she slapped that bad-boy on the boardroom table and watched as the middle-managers cowered in their minimalist, post-modern chairs.

(Before the huddle, Marissa bounced her idea off her cube-mate Janelle. Janelle told her the idea was terrible but then presented it to the team at the meeting as her own. Marissa was too mortified to accuse her outright and simply said, 'Great idea you had, Janelle,' in a way she hoped sounded a bit sarcastic – but not overly so – because Jack, their manager was listening. After the meeting, Marissa did not call her mother in Anigonish even though she wanted to. Instead, she sat with the phone in her hand and told herself to breathe.)

"MARIKA"

Marika is a cobra; precise and deadly. She smells subterfuge from fifty yards and strikes without remorse. After

Janelle's betrayal, Marika stalked that duplicitous toad into the women's lavatory, and devoured her whole.

(Later, when Janelle started bragging to Jeff from I.T. about 'her' great idea, Marissa felt a panic attack coming on. She rushed to the washroom and while she was in there her doing her deep breathing, Janelle came in to apply more lipstick. Unable to contain herself, Marissa asked Janelle how she could stand herself and Janelle told Marissa to keep her voice down and maybe get some counselling while she was at it. When she got back to her desk, Marissa did call her mother in Antigonish and told her a story that was mostly Marika's version of things. Her mother said 'That's my honey-pie. Don't let the city girls get you down,' and Marissa felt somewhat better.)

"MERISHA"

Merisha may look tame to the untrained eye, but she is directly descended from Actual Goddamn Amazons. She would sooner cut off her right breast than tolerate the chauvinist bull-crap of her manager Jack, so when Jack suggested he take Merisha and Janelle out for coffee so they could 'talk it out,' Merisha called him on it, hard and fast. She got right up in Jack's face and asked him if he would approach a legitimate workplace dispute between two *male* colleges with the same 'Why don't you two girls go get a coffee and learn to play nice' sort of way? No? Didn't think so, Jackass.

(After Janelle refused to go to the coffee shop, Jack suggested he and Marissa go alone. While he sipped his Half-Caf Soy Latte, Jack let his hand linger on Marissa's forearm in a way she felt was too familiar and said 'a little bird told him' Marissa might be having some personal issues that were spilling over into her work life. After that, Jack told Marissa he thought she looked 'really svelte' in her new skirt. When it was time to go back up to the office, Marissa told Jack to go on ahead and stayed back in the coffee shop to 'get one to go.' When she called her mother in Antigonish from the coffee shop's washroom and told her how things went down with Merisha and Jack, Marissa's mother said

14

'that ought to give that character a thing or two to chew on,' but this time it did not make Marissa feel much better. Then Marissa's mother casually mentioned the weekend 'Lady Leaders Course' that their old neighbour Darla was teaching at Dalhousie and wondered aloud how long it would take Marissa to drive there from her apartment on a Saturday, when there was no traffic.)

"ALISSA"

Alissa is a tiny piece of jalapeno who hides in your Spicy Chorizo Breakfast Sandwich. If you bite into her, she will set your whole damn world on fire. When Alissa was on her way back to the elevators, she noticed Jack standing at the security desk trying to throw his weight around with Venka, the Agent on Duty. Alissa, never one to let a sister down, marched right up to the desk and together she and Venka proceeded to roast Jack like the lightweight marshmallow he was.

(Marissa, unsure of what to do about bearing witness to the escalating situation between Jack and Venka, hovered uncomfortably in the general vicinity of the security desk and watched as Jack demanded to know who the hell Venka thought she was. Jack then informed Venka she was just some tattooed dumb ass in a fake cop uniform and he was goddamned if she was going to dictate where the Manager of Marketing went in his own place of work. Venka stood up from her chair and told Jack he had exactly five fucking seconds to apologize and when he didn't, Venka reached over, laid her palms flat on his pectorals, and told him to back the hell up. Jack turned and stomped off toward the elevators but Marissa hung back just long enough to lean into Venka's ear and whisper 'Venka, I have never once admired a human being more than I do you right now.')

"MARYSA"

Marysa is a secret agent of the Republic of Whoop-ass and she's trained to maim. If you cross her, she'll take you down like nineteen-seventies wallpaper. Jack thought his troubles were over once he fled the security desk, but Marysa was just getting started. When she was leaving for the day, she backed her 2021 canary-yellow Porche 911 into Jack's entry-level BMW and burned rubber out of the parking lot. She lifted her clenched fist through the open sunroof and sped off into the hot afternoon, daring any of those corporate ass-clowns to follow her.

(After Marissa returned to her cubicle, Jack called her into his office. He said he was sorry she had had to witness that ugliness at the Security Desk, especially since today was such an 'emotional day' for her. While he said this, Jack pressed his knee against Marissa's thigh under the desk and slipped his fingers across the hem of her skirt. At that point, everything started to cave in around Marissa. She knew the panic attack of the century was coming on, so she backed out of Jack's office, grabbed the keys to her mother's hand-me-down 1999 Corolla, and headed down to the parking garage. In her desperation to flee the building, she miscalculated her exit from the parking space and accidentally hit the front fender of Jack's car. She leapt from her car to assess the damage and stood like a tortured stone angel as the last drops of her reserve crashed to the concrete floor. Suddenly, the voice of Venka echoed through the grey walls of the garage. 'Just drive,' Venka said. 'I've already deleted the footage. I won't have a job here tomorrow anyway, so what the fuck? Don't let the bastards get you down.'

Marissa stared into the security camera that was right next to her and mouthed 'Thank you' into the lens. As she left the parking garage, Marissa put her hand through the sunroof to wave at Venka in case she was still watching. That night, and for many nights after, Marissa did not call her mother. Eventually her mother drove down from Antigonish. Marissa answered the door in her bathrobe and her mother said, 'Tell me all about it, love, every last bit,' but Marissa wasn't ready to talk yet, so she just stood there in the doorway and let her mother hold her.)

"AIKO"

Aiko is a modern-day Wonder Woman and she's ready to smash right through the glass ceiling. She heard the girl she replaced had some sort of nervous breakdown but Aiko is not going to let herself meet the same fate. On her third week of work Aiko noticed a note scrawled on the inside of the cardboard heat-sleeve of her Caramel No-Foam Macchiato.

'If you want to survive this shark-tank, please note the following:

1) There is a toad lurking in the cubicle beside you. She will betray you.
2) Your manager has fast hands and a penchant for gaslighting. Take notes. There are human rights laws in this country that are about to blow his friggin' mind.
3) Caffeine is a terrible cure for anxiety.
4) Don't ever lie to your mother, she can see right through you.
5) If you require backup, Dalhousie's Certificate in Women's leadership is taught by a kickass woman named Darla. Registration for the next session closes in 8 weeks.
6) Marissa, the somewhat aggressive new barista at the coffee shop is your ally. She and her roommate Venka are saving up to enroll in the course at Dal. Tip her well and often.
7) Don't let the bastards get you down.'

The All Of It, It Misses You, Come Home
by Sheena Cook Kopman

Winner, Edinburgh Award for Flash Fiction 2023

The farm misses you, the wind in the barley misses you, the combine rolling home with your dad inside it, the burn water you paddled in with your brother, the grass under the crabapple tree where you made daisy chains and played croquet, the gooseberry bushes your grandfather planted, the view from your bedroom over the lambs across the field to the top road where the school bus goes, the secret room off your bedroom where your grandmother hid her letters, the grandmother clock at the top of the back stairs, the piano with the music open where you left it, the box of wine on the fridge so your dad could pour a glass without getting up, the round kitchen table with your brother s spelling pressed into it, the blue milk jug with its beaded cover, the ginger cat asleep by the Raeburn, the potatoes in the red basin, the needles in the tomato pincushion on the windowsill for splinters in your hand, the gooseberry jam on the larder shelf, your mother s handwriting on the label, your dad s wellingtons and heartbreaking socks and growing collection of walking sticks, the stone water trough you sat on with your brother when you brought him his tea and warm roly-poly, your grandmother s faded pink roses around the kitchen window, heads heavy with raindrops, the stroll around the farm you never got to take with her. The all of it, it misses you. Come home, we ll bring you over the water, come home.

Life Goes On
by Jonathan Sellars

Second Prize, Edinburgh Award for Flash Fiction 2023

When I died the first time I came back as a muntjac deer, which was a surprise. I actually started laughing. It was ironic you see, given I'd been swerving to avoid one. Then a dog bit my leg. I bloody hate dogs. The bone stuck out sideways and it hurt like hell. The laughing stopped.

I did worry I wouldn't come back a second time, but I couldn't live as a three-legged muntjac. No one could. My initial plan was to wander down the A52 until someone put me out of my misery. But I didn't. Not because I was scared, I just hated the thought of a driver making the same mistake I had, avoiding the small squidgy deer only to hit the big hard tree. I didn't want the blood of a surgeon rushing to a life-saving operation, or even a slightly irritating estate agent, on my hoofs. Of course, the unlucky driver might have been a corrupt politician or an adulterous bastard, but I reasoned they weren't the swerving type.

Eventually I found a fox who'd do the job. It seemed a no brainer, a free meal plus a couple of days off hunting to do whatever foxes do in their free time. Sex, probably. But the first few I approached were reluctant, didn't agree with the euthanistic nature of my request. That's foxes for you I guess.

Anyway, now I'm a chaffinch and I fly around crapping on dogs all day. Life's great.

Hot Wind
by Mandy Wheeler

Second Prize, Edinburgh Short Story Award 2023

Hello Dad,

It's been a while. Can you remember the last time I wrote to you? Neither can I. It was probably when I was at school. You didn't answer then, so this won't be so different.

I thought you'd want to know I finally made it to see the solicitor today, the one who's handling your will. I said I wouldn't, but I did, so that's one up to you already. I see you've gone for the cheap option as usual. That solicitor is a fool. He's got a cocky manner and he wears bad shoes. At one point he even called me 'Charlie'. He explained the conditions of the bequest like I was an idiot. He actually giggled when he handed me the envelope, then said, *'Here's your mission should you wish to accept it,'* in an American accent. He told me he blamed Orson Wells for this kind of thing. 'You know, Rosebud and all that.' When I said, 'This kind of thing' was hardly common practice,' he rolled his eyes and said, 'You'd be surprised.'

I locked the paperwork away in a drawer as soon as I got home. I shall bin it tomorrow. I won't let you bully me from beyond the grave. I won't. You can keep your money.

Peter and Tom are coming round tonight. Yes, that Peter. I'm making asparagus quiche. That's right, quiche.

You'll be glad to know the quiche was a success. The rest of the evening was pretty depressing. Peter and Tom brought a bottle of fizz to toast 'the end of an era'. They meant you. I didn't join in. Then Peter went off on one about me being 'in denial' about the bequest. I hate it when Peter does his 'I know you so well' act. It reminds me of you. I'm not his responsibility anymore.

I got a call from Peter this morning. Apparently Tom has decided 'the task'—that's what he calls it—is a crossword clue. He says, *'Hot Wind to be returned to Maker'* is the kind of thing you get in The Times. That makes sense. The nursing home said you did The Times crossword every morning, right up to the end. According to Tom, 'Hot Wind' is an anagram and 'To be returned' means you read it backwards, or insert the letter R, or something. The answer will be a word that means 'Maker'. The capital letters are a mislead, apparently. But, of course, you already know all that. And you know I don't. Remember you tried to teach me to do crosswords when I was a kid? You decided I 'didn't have the right kind of brain'. One more disappointment for you. I'd forgotten about that. Thanks for reminding me.

An email has arrived from the little squirt in the solicitor's office. Do I think I will be fulfilling the terms of the bequest and claiming the money? I've deleted it. You will not do this to me. Peter thinks I'm being selfish. He says even if I don't need the money for myself—which of course he knows I do, and so did you—I could give it away to a good cause. He's got some journalist at The Times who could put me in touch with their crossword setter to help me out. He says this guy 'Owes him a favour.' I bet he does.

I didn't sleep last night. I keep wondering—what happens if I solve the puzzle? Does the solicitor just hand over a cheque? I can't believe you'd make it that easy. Tom thinks it'll turn out to be treasure hunt. He 'adores' treasure hunts apparently. Tom can be terribly childish sometimes. I don't know how Peter puts up with it. Anyway, I don't think it's a treasure hunt—more likely some kind of challenge. That's more your style. Jerking me around with lots of demeaning little tasks, things you know I'll fail at, things to prove I'm still not 'brave'. Or perhaps you'll

21

go straight for the big one, demand I find a nice girl and settle down.

A box arrived this morning. I didn't answer the university's email inviting me to clear out your office, so they've done it for me. It's not a very big box. I won't open it.

I've found it. I've found Hot Wind. Not a crossword clue, but a painting. A rather good painting, in fact. A landscape with a single, square building, almost lost in a yellow haze. It was in the box from the university. Peter demanded I 'stop being a coward' and open the damn thing.

Tom noticed the title 'Hot Wind' written in the bottom corner and a signature: 'T. Hunt, 1947'. He said the yellow haze reminded him of a sandstorm he and Peter saw when they were on holiday in Tunisia. We found the piece of paper stuck on the back too—the name Timothy Hunt and an address in Suffolk. That's your handwriting, isn't it?

Hot Wind to be returned to its Maker. Ok Dad, I get it.

This business with the painting has spooked me. Unless you've changed dramatically in the decades since I last saw you, there's something odd about it. You despised art. I should know, I'm the one whose plans to go to art school you pissed on. And this is a skillful painting, not an amateur daub. What was it doing in your office? I spoke to Karen, your secretary. She says you brought it with you when you joined the university. She remembers it hanging above your desk. So why do I have to return it? Did you steal it or something? Or did you fiddle the artist out of money, beat the price down to get a bargain. That's more your style.

Ok, I've sent a letter. I don't know why I'm bothering. Timothy Hunt is probably dead by now. He certainly won't be at the same address. I didn't go into detail, just put in a photo of the painting and said you wanted it returned to the artist. Didn't mention that there was a hundred grand for me riding on it.

I've just received an email from a woman called Rosie Sullivan. She says she's Timothy Hunt's daughter. The Suffolk address was the family home, sold when her father went into a home a couple of years ago. He's still alive but it sounds like he's not in a good way. And he's not an artist, he's an engineer. She's going to take the photo next time she visits. What the hell is all this about, Dad?

I've had more messages from Rosie Sullivan. She's asked me to visit and bring the picture, as soon as possible. When I didn't reply immediately, she wrote again wanting to know when I intend to come. She says it's important that I come quickly, says her father was very distressed when he saw the photo of the painting.

I can see Rosie Sullivan won't leave me alone until I go, so I've booked a train ticket for Monday morning. I'm hooked now, aren't I? You've got me. I wish I'd stuck to my resolve and ignored the damn bequest like I promised myself I would. Poor impulse control, that's what you used to call it.

Peter rang and offered to come with me. He said he could tell I was feeling anxious about it all. I snapped and told him that my emotions are nothing to do with him anymore. And anyway, this is something I have to do on my own, isn't it? Finally.

I need to write this down.

He was sitting in a chair when we arrived, rocking back and forward. A little old man with a brown rug over his legs. He didn't look at us but almost snatched the painting out of my hands. Then he stared at it for ages without saying a word. When his daughter asked if the painting was his, he just nodded.

She pointed to the date and asked if it was somewhere he was stationed in the War. When I said that my friend thought it might be Tunisia, he let out a yelp at the sound of my voice, as though he was in pain. Then he leant forward and grabbed my head between his hands and stared at my face. Then, God help us, he started to cry.

I left immediately. I didn't want to embarrass the poor man or his daughter any further. Just as I was pulling out of the car park, the daughter ran up and pushed a supermarket carrier bag through the car window. She was very insistent that I take it. Told me to call her 'when I was ready.' All the way home in the car, I could still hear that old man's sobbing.

I've left the bag in my car. It's full of letters. I recognise your handwriting.

I've read them.

I had a couple of drinks last night then worked my way through the bag. I read them all. All your letters. Your love letters. Your sexy, intense love letters. Your love letters to him, to Timothy. You and Timothy. Timothy and you.

I can't believe I have just written those lines.

It's after the war. You write every day: he's in Suffolk, you're in London. You write about the places you've been together, the things you've seen. You tell Timothy you meet him in your dreams. In one letter, you remind him of a sandstorm you were caught in together—how it blinded everyone so that 'for once we did not have to hide what we were doing.' You tell Timothy Hunt that you cannot live without him.

In later letters you're making plans. You want to live with Timothy. You say: 'We'll find a way.' Hah! Now that's a line I recognise. A line used by so many of what you would later sneeringly refer to as 'that sort'. Meaning my sort.

And then, for no apparent reason, you stop writing. What happened Dad, did your father find out?

24

It's been a week now since I visited the care home. An envelope arrived this morning from Rosie Sullivan. After I left, her father attacked the painting and tore the canvas. A letter fell out of the back, addressed to you, in Timothy Hunt's handwriting.

So, Dad, I know. I've read the letter in which Timothy tells you he has changed his mind. That he can't go through with it; can't face what being together will bring. He says he knows he is not brave—not like you. He tells you that he has started seeing a nice girl who teaches at the local school and is thinking of settling down. He says her name is Carole, he thinks you'd like her. He says he is sorry, so very sorry. I cried when I read that letter, Dad. For both of us.

30TH April. Timothy Hunt died last night, two weeks after 'Hot Wind' was returned to its maker. Rosie plans to have the picture mended, she wants to keep it. She didn't know her father could paint. Something else he gave up. I got a bit carried away and suggested we could use the money from the bequest to open a little art gallery, somewhere near the beach in Suffolk. I've got this idea that we could license the place; that Tom and Peter could get married there. I really want to believe you'd like that, Dad, that you wanted me to discover all this, that I wasn't just being used as a delivery boy to your old lover. But I'll never know, will I?

Rosie says if we do ever open the gallery, we should hang 'Hot Wind' in the window, in memory of you both. She says it would be a start. I hope it might be an end. We'll see.

Goodbye Dad,
Your son. Charles.

Join Hands
by Sean Gill

Third Prize, Edinburgh Award for Flash Fiction 2023

Truthfully they learned Morse code so that, while holding hands at the opera, they could squeeze secret messages to each other about the *Barber of Seville*'s sweat stains or the woman in the royal box who looked like a flamingo, but more often than not it was simply, *ti amo* or *vita mia*, because ninety minutes between intermissions felt like forever, *per sempre*, far too long not to say *I love you, you are my life*.

They had been married thirteen years when they joined the anti-fascist *arditi*. Their comrades marveled at their constant affection and inability to withstand the slightest separation. They joked, 'He still kisses her like yesterday's bride!'

The Code was useful in this new life, and on missions to Athens, or Marseille, their secret dispatches were sprinkled with *amore mio*s and *ti adoro*s.

OVRA agents picked them up at Ciampino airport. Blindfolded and gagged, they were thrown into a van, destination unknown.

When they heard the crashing waves, they wondered if they'd arrived at a cliffside to be cast off and drowned. Or perhaps a coastal prison, where they would surely be separated. Two fates. Both deaths.

Neither had yet used the Code. He wanted to squeeze a novel's worth of adulation onto her hand in dots and dashes. She squeezed, *you are the very best thing*, and he managed to repeat it. They held each other like lovers from Pompeii, tightly, like they were defying death, like they always had.

The solar system
by Drew Taylor

Winner, The Golden Hare Award 2023
Shortlisted, Edinburgh Award for Flash Fiction 2023

Look up in the sky. There! That's my dad on his way to Jupiter with his pals. He's a physicist. His specialism is plasma physics. What's plasma physics? Haven't a clue. When I asked, he told me I'm too young to understand.

Standing next to me at the window, doing the washing up, is Mum. She's a mother. Her specialism is me. She says she knows all there is to know about me because she's my mother, whereas Dad, she says, is still getting to grips with plasma physics, like everything else.

Observing us from his basket in the corner is our black cat, Oscar. His specialism is catching mice he brings in at night then releases. He's a useless article, according to Mum and Dad. I admire how he sees everything but says nothing.

That's Mister Gordon from next door sitting at the kitchen table. He's just given me money to go out and spend on anything I want. His specialism is fixing things when Dad's not around. I overheard Mum tell him he 'has the magic touch.'

Outside, drawing up in her car, is Mrs Gordon. She left a short while ago to drive to her yoga class. She must have forgotten something. Her specialism is divorce law. She's divorced more couples than she cares to remember, she once told me. Mister Gordon, being an accountant, must count his lucky stars.

Finally, there's me: the son. Everyone revolves around me. My specialism is keeping them in the dark.

The Clear Out
by Patrick McLoughlin

Third Prize, Edinburgh Short Story Award 2023

Time changes most things they say. Accept the changes of time. Embrace the turning of the world. Appreciate the seasons. Watch the everyday carefully. Let the simple moments become as big as you want them to be. I do all these things. I don't need lessons to tell me how.

Mary Nagle drinks her tea in my kitchen. She eyes the sofa that she would have thrown out twenty years ago, the half of the table taken up with letters from agricultural departments, bills, vet's receipts, solicitor's letters, and flyers from election campaigns that carried on without my input, calf tags and antibiotic bottles, all piled on each other making no order or sense to her. She offers advice and every word sounds and has always sounded like a judgement. I know there's a smell. Off the house. Off me. The house is the farm. The farm is the house. The farm is me. I am the farm.

It is August already. After six weeks of only the odd bit of fine mist barely enough to wet a sheet of toilet paper, of passing dark clouds refusing to open up, it finally poured last night, so much so, that at one stage I thought a lake would run under the back door. I walked around earlier this morning in the back field and could feel the soil give a little under my feet. I could almost see little movements in the grass as it tried to reach upwards. I've long stopped telling people that we could do with rain. There seems to me to be two types of people left around here, and possibly the world, but the world as it is, in the sense of the outside world, doesn't bother me and until now I had no interest in bothering it.

The world as I know it is this. Grass clipped to its heel with all its colour burned dry. A lame cow and a scoury calf.

Those are the things that make my heart ache. Healthy cows, strong thirsty calves, warm milk in black buckets, me, my sheds, and my bit of land. These are things that make it leap. Within a week I will see the change the rain has brought. The animals and I will do what we do. Time will move on and I will notice it all. This is the world I know and the only world I care to know.

'You can head up to Dublin anytime you like, stay in fine hotels, eat in all those restaurants reviewed in weekend magazines, buy all the clothes you feel like. You can travel in comfort and get a top of the range car. Take in a play or something, treat yourself.' I stand in the middle of my kitchen waiting for her to finish her tea and get up and be gone home to her husband who she'll bore with the same old talk about my stained mugs.

'Why in blazes would I drive all the way to Dublin to eat my dinner?'

'Jesus, Jean! It's not about the dinner! It's about seeing what's out there. You can do anything you want. You're free. Embrace it.'

'I'm going to skin a rabbit now, Mary, right here in this basin, so you'd probably not want to be around when I start.'

Donal McLaughlin comes weekly and we sometimes go into town to look at what he calls the new developments. Last Tuesday we took a look at the building works on the Kilduff side of town. Apartments. Two and three bedroom.

'They'll be fine jobs altogether, Jean. I could put your name down for one. Close to the shops. Lots of neighbours if you have a fall or anything. It would suit you grand. Even if you don't decide to live in it you could rent it out. In fact, you could probably buy five or six of them. No animals to tend. No carting muck from sheds. No watching calving cows in the middle of winter. You could have a second life as a landlady. What do you think of that?'

Four years ago, a hurricane passed over the country and the red warnings went up for the entire nation. By one in the

29

afternoon, all work had stopped in every county and parents and children were brought together in the middle of the working week like a test run for a future calamity. The next day on the radio it was clear that three deaths weren't enough to warrant the interruptions to people's comings and goings. It's as if the air itself will turn solid if we pause for even a moment. The beauty of living in the countryside with fields of your own is best seen on those days. The towns, the cities and the roads are full of dangers. A flying bin can kill. A tree can crush a car. But in the middle of a field, there is nothing that can hurt you. I went out there on that day and lay down on the grass and closed my eyes. It felt like I was at once part of the storm and completely removed from it, as if I was in the womb of nature, aware of its force yet protected by it. I looked at the clouds being pushed along by the roar and knew with all my heart that this was the sky that I wanted to die under.

Brian O' Mahony has seen the eggshells on my kitchen floor, tea bags in the sink, spoons with sugar welded to the metal, a bread board full of crumbs and old onion skins left beside a heel of white loaf. He sees me as a lump covered in a green wax coat and wellies. Your little calving shed is in better shape than this place, he'd say. I'm surprised you don't have framed pictures of them on the walls in there. He can be a bit of a bollix but he helps out and understands me, and for that, I like him, even if most can't stand him.

'You know, I've heard of women like you,' he said last week, bent low, arse crack showing, squeezing the curds of mastitis out of a back left tit. 'And what they do is head off to Asia or India or that area anyway and hook up with a young lad. You'd pay him, like, a bit to keep him sweet, I dunno how much, but he'd be like a comfort blanket to you, always there for you, protecting you and praising you and tucking you into bed, pretending to love you and all you have to do is imagine it's real and for a lot of people, Jean, imagining that isn't so hard when they are looking for a bit of comfort.'

30

'I could pay you for that,' I said. 'I wouldn't have to travel far then.'

'You can pay me to milk these girls here and we'll be grand.'

There seems to me to be two types of people. There are those like me that hope for rain when we feel the ground could do with it. Do I want to see everything remain the same? Maybe some things. Healthy rivers and green grass. But even more I want to see the world keep turning and changing the way that natural time intends and watch it from a seat I know.

The machines are coming. They'll start with clearing the stone walls and the hedgerows and the hawthorn bushes probably. The rabbits will scamper and return confused. A half day and the place will be unrecognizable. Then the sheds and the house and the levelling of the land all nice and smooth and flat. Four years of hounding. Take the money. Accept the change. You are free. More than you can ever spend. Work for the area and new beginnings. What were you getting out of it anyway?

I read once that the average modern American makes as many as three big changes during their adult life. A new job on the edge of a different ocean. Bad marriages. Looking for warmer climates as the bones get thin. Losing everything. Starting over. I know a local woman who lost her home through floods when she was seventy four. Moved into town. Walked concrete instead of grass. James Bradley died one week after his wife. No reason to continue. The average American would be just getting going, but some of us aren't put here for that.

The machines are parked all along the wall of the first field behind my sheds. None of the men stopped by my door. I've already got the instructions. Four weeks to vacate the house. You're dragging it out said Mary. I'll fix you up with some lovely furniture said Donal. Have you organised a lover boy said Brian. I am, Mary. Do that, Donal. I have, Brian.

31

I could change. I could change if I wanted to. If that was what I wanted, if it was somehow my choice.

I thought about lying under one of them as they burned. The second one – after the first was lit and let the next one take me with it. But I couldn't just destroy for the sake of it. All of those machines could easily be replaced and I couldn't leave with that kind of act on my conscience. Smoke and ash pouring into the sky for no reason, choking birds and blackening the land.

I have never cleared my hedgerows or trees or scrubby parts. They run the border of every field and house most of the area's wildlife. I don't blame other people for shaving their land clean, looking for every extra inch of grass to feed ten more stock, always hoping that they catch up with what the offices call progress. I am the one who progress has now chased and run over. In a flash, everything will go.

Sleeping outdoors is not something I am familiar with. For all my love of the land and sky, I have always been the caretaker and not one of the creatures that I tend. Their place was theirs and mine was mine. It is my biggest regret, all of a sudden, even though a week ago it had never crossed my mind. What was my bed for anyway? Only for sleeping. Shutting out the day and folding up myself in preparation for the next. I have seen many moons but how many have I really noticed? I am fully covered here in my new bed under the bushes. A child could spend a week hiding in here and not be found. Will I sleep? Will I be sleeping when the machines roar through? I doubt it. For now, I take in the smell of the earth and the sounds of the night that have always been here but never heard and will never be heard again.

There seems to me to be two types of people. To those that would rather burn under a constant sun for what they think is the ideal, all I can think is that they must be blinded by its glare.

Partners
by Penny-Anne Beaudoin

Commendation, Edinburgh Award for Flash Fiction 2023

An old friend she hasn't seen in years visits our table. He asks her to dance and she blushes, *blushes*, and looks to me. For permission, I guess. I shrug. She takes it as a yes. He offers his hand, helps her up, and even before they reach the dancefloor, she's in his arms.

And god, oh god, oh god, she dances like a pro, like she's been doing it all her life. But we *never* dance. Well, a few shuffles around the floor at our wedding, but that's all. So, when did she learn *this*? And how is it, after all these years, I never knew?

Her hand rests lightly on his shoulder, his in the small of her back. Everyone stops to watch them own the floor, the music, each other. The way he… what's the word?… *partners* her, leads her, even lifts her at one point. Not over his head or anything like that, but just enough her feet leave the floor for a moment and god, oh god, oh god, it feels like someone's crushing my throat, and I hope I'm still man enough not to break down right here, in front of everybody.

They sweep past my table and I see his mouth form a word, a question.

'Remember?' he says, his lips almost touching her ear. She blushes again, smiles, and leans in to whisper something back, just as he turns her away from me.

Keep your filthy damn hands
by Amy Edmunds

Commendation, Edinburgh Award for Flash Fiction 2023

'Keep your filthy damn hands to yourself!' she'd yelled. No, hissed — loud enough to stir every soul in the carriage.

Even the noise-cancelled ones.

But then again, not too loud. Not enough to attract their scorn. She was a professional, not a madwoman. Assertive, not deranged.

He'd recoiled, shocked. Shame boiling up red as all eyes turned and bore into him.

He must have thought he'd settled on a meek-looking one. Boy did he get that wrong.

People had tutted, glared, bubbled up with judgment, with contempt for this sorry loser who couldn't control his straying, deviant hands. They'd offered her glances of delicious complicity, rolling skyward, and together they had ridden the wave of outrage until it set them back safe on their civil, law-abiding feet.

On the other hand, maybe she'd sworn. Maybe it was better to let the anger rip. Yes, that felt good, that was better, and the people had rallied around her. One had squared up to him, threatened a punch.

He'd regret today's casual act of frottage, would this coward.

She saturates the tints, sharpens the edges, mixes the audio just so.

She is a master of post-production. A dab hand at deep fake in the cutting room of her mind.

So much so that she is sometimes able to forget that she'd simply let it go, swallowed her fire, tamed that thumping pulse. Avoided a scene.

That he'd alighted, unruffled, at his station, the thrill of her cotton skirt still on his palm.

The Survivor
by Dorothy Coe

Winner, Isobel Lodge Award 2023
Shortlisted for the 2023 Edinburgh Short Story Award

'Mr MacInnes, what would you say was the cause of this tragedy?' asked Mr Anderson of the Marine Accident Investigation Branch.

No one else was left to tell the tale. No-one to tell it differently.

No-one. Victor MacInnes couldn't get the haunting images out of his mind, even now, two years later. Every time he closed his eyes to seek sleep, he saw the wide-open, terrified eyes of Cammie, clinging white-knuckled, to the already half-submerged starboard side of the listing Samphire, every muscle straining, but unable to force himself upward against gravity and momentum, as another merciless 20-foot wave smashed into the wheelhouse, sucking the boat down and Cammie with it. Victor could feel again the power of the sea, sweeping him up, the cold, the confusion. Then he would shout out involuntarily, as he had then 'Get up! Get out! Sandy! Yan! Robbie! Save yersells.' But they couldn't get up. They had gone below to rest, exhausted after 48 hours fishing, hauling, landing, gutting, and stowing fish boxes. Drowned before anyone above knew what was happening. Gone to rest. Unlike Victor, who knew he could never rest again.

Desperate to sleep, his ears were filled with the confused cries of his crew competing with the shrieks of the gulls that always met them when they were near to home. How could they be so near home and yet so far? His fingers scrabbled uncontrollably, unconsciously trying again in vain to send the mayday message, confounded by the loss of the boat's electrical power and radio signal as the sea finally overwhelmed the wheelhouse.

Afterwards, when he had to relive it all for the Marine Accident Investigation Branch, the guilt of surviving when his crew perished was as hard to bear as the grief for his lost friends. But what could he tell Mr Anderson?

The kid, Robbie, always on about his wee one – only two and his pride and joy. His mind only half on the job once the herring were stowed, desperate to get home. His job it was to count the boxes stowed in the hold (410 – a good catch) and then secure the hatches on the fish hold below the working deck. The fish hold, out of sight of the wheelhouse, where that day, the hatch covers, carelessly unsecured, had let in the sea when the storm blew up, rapidly filling up with seawater, critically reducing the stability of the boat as she heaved in the swell, causing her to heel disastrously and irrevocably.

Sandy and Yan, unaware, in the cabin below, with the doors open so they could exchange banter about the Poland-Scotland friendly till they fell asleep, Yan teasing Sandy yet again about all the football games he'd go to when he retired in a month's time when Sandy would by then be a married man with a tight collar and leash on him. The weathertight doors that, properly closed, would have prevented the ingress of seawater into the engine room and lower cabin and might have given them vital seconds to escape the doomed vessel.

Cammie, the watchkeeper at the crucial time, always after the skipper's job – 'Just wait till ah get ma papers. Ye'll no see me for spray. That'll be me on the big boaties then' –who, alone on watch, with everyone sleeping, in deteriorating conditions, recognised that something was amiss, even though he didn't know what, but didn't call his skipper. 'Ah can dae it. It's a breeze. Naething tae it.' Except he couldn't. The change in the weather, the unseen loose covers on the fish hold and the hidden flooding there, the sudden, unexpected loss of power and radio signal as the water swamped the engine room. All conspired to rob him of the chance at his skipper's certificate.

And Victor. The skipper. The violent lurch of the Samphire had roused him instantly from his sleep in his cabin, then slipping and sliding along the deck, he burst into the already half-submerged wheelhouse, Robbie right behind him. He tried and failed to send the mayday, as the electrics cut out, shouting at them all to get out. Then, he was swept helplessly by the force of the crashing wave. The same wave that took Cammie and Robbie down, sent Victor upwards, spinning crazily, not knowing up from down, by chance not choice, out of the port wheelhouse window, left open when it should have been closed. Luck or a curse? Into the open sea with only the automatically launched life raft for company. How often did he dive down looking for Robbie and the others, surely just behind him still, until exhausted and ice-cold he clambered alone into the inflatable and found the thermal blanket and the emergency flare.

So when Mr Anderson of the Marine Accident Investigation Branch asked Victor, 'Mr MacInnes, what would you say was the cause of this tragedy?' what could he say? He'd had to look Cammie's ma in the eye. And Sandy's fiancée. And Yan's brother. Hostile accusation staring back at him. Worst of all, he'd had to face Robbie's wee girl, still putting her hand trustingly in his, before her mother snatched it away. How could he tell them the truth?

So, no. Not their fault, none of them. The story of their deaths should remain untainted by blame.

The ship's owner, his faither, so proud thirty-odd years ago of a new-born son after 5 daughters, that he broke with family naming conventions and gave him the name Victor, instead of the traditional Andrew, patron saint of the fishermen. It was tempting fate, his granny said so. Generations of brave MacInnes fishermen had been protected by the name of their ancestor – a charm not to be lightly cast aside. 'Pride that dines wi vanity sups wi contempt,' she warned.

His faither, too old now to go to sea himself, grieved for the Samphire, the boat he'd spent his life savings to buy, and the loss of his pride in his son. His faither had not spoken to him once since the sinking: a true skipper goes down with his ship, doesn't he? His faither, who had laughingly ridiculed Vic's plea to fix the broken bilge alarm that would have alerted the crew to gathering water in the fish hold and the engine room. 'New-fangled gizmos. Just cause more trouble. We hud naethin the like o that in ma day,' he'd said, testily. 'But dinna ye fash yersel, son. Ah'll get the ingineer on that as soon as ye're back.'

Victor felt the estrangement from his faither as keenly as the loss of his crew, but accepted it, almost welcomed it, as his just punishment for surviving. No, Faither could not be blamed either.

Leaving the enquiry, he caught sight of his reflection in the glass door and saw a stranger – gaunt face with dark circles below the eyes, hat pulled down, collar turned up to prevent recognition in the town where everyone knew his shame.

No one, least of all he himself, celebrated his survival. He didn't drown, but his life was over.

Alice under the table
by Jane Broughton

Commendation, Edinburgh Award for Flash Fiction 2023

A lice was in her hiding place, under the gateleg table, hidden by a heavy cloth. Humming to herself, she arranged her grandmother's miniature ceramic animals in order of ferocity – mouse, hedgehog, peacock, otter. None of them were as ferocious as Grandma. Grandma would be the sharp toothed old fox.

Alice watched as Grandma popped peas with the practised precision of an assassin. Grandad had brought a bag of pods from the allotment. He'd tipped them onto an old oilcloth, its worn sheen reflecting rays of the setting sun like a golden pool. Her Grandma had sighed as she scooped them into the colander. He'd reached out a hand to help but she'd batted him away.

'Be off with you now, Albert, wash those hands. Our Alice doesn't need any encouragement to be slovenly.'

Alice, feeling invincible in her den, stuck her tongue out and returned to the animals, debating whether a rabbit or a squirrel would win in a fight to the death.

Grandad returned and held his hands out for inspection. He's like a little mouse, Alice thought scornfully.

Then, with a conjuror's flourish, he reached into a faded Co-op bag and produced a posy of candy-coloured wildflowers. Alice was surprised to see Grandma's flushed cheeks. Grandma stroked the velvet petals and looked into her husband's eyes.

Alice returned to the animals. She moved the mouse to the front. Then she emerged from her lair.

Her Grandad grinned at her and disappeared behind the newspaper.

To the new neighbour three doors down who steals my strawberries
by Marie Gethins

Commendation, Edinburgh Award for Flash Fiction 2023

Perhaps you once gathered them in a forest, rubies cast among emerald leaves, or haggled with a fruit seller in Sevastopol or Kherson or Odesa, their sweetness grown under glass as an early spring treat.

Perhaps you recall that taste of joy and the promise of other harvests when sunflower fields turn their pebbled faces to the sun. A time for making preserves, jars stacked on sturdy shelves, so in winter the scent and taste of warmer times can be spread thick on bread, shared round a family table.

Perhaps you see beloved in the damaged berries, cradled for an extra moment. A pause and facial shift, maybe you recall blackened apartment shells, twisted bodies in the street. Standing alone in morning stillness, perhaps you hear an echo of sirens and cluster bombs. In these moments, my breathing stops until another one is plucked.

While you try to navigate among foreign tongue and unfamiliar tastes, I tend these beds with extra care and whisper *more, more, more,* hoping your dawn hands will find release in what little I can offer.

Table 22
by Kate Anderson

Winner, Write Mango Short Story Award 2023
Shortlisted for the Edinburgh Short Story Award 2023

R ae arrived a little before seven just as the moon was rising full and bright in the sky. The steps down to the restaurant were slippery underfoot and her heels clacked on the stone as she descended. She pulled open the door and was hit with the rush of noise and heat.

Lupo's was heaving.

In the toilets she washed her hands in water that alternated between lukewarm and scalding and considered the distinct possibility that this evening could go one of two ways; the instantaneous 'ick' – as had been the disappointing first impression of lolloping Steve; or, much worse than that perhaps, was the crushing prospect that *her date* would be perfect… but that *she* would not… She applied a little powder to her face and patted at the fly-away hairs that were lifting in all directions in a bizarre 'Van de Graph' halo around her head.

She fished in her bag for her phone.

I'm here. Absolutely terrified. Wish me luck! xx

She pressed send. A message buzzed almost immediately in response.

Got everything crossed for you doll!

And beneath that a line of aubergine emojis.

******

Weaving their way through the densely packed tables and towards the farthest end of the restaurant, Rae had the distinctly uncomfortable sense that she was being watched by everyone in the room. A man twisting a long strand of tagliatelle paused with his fork in mid air and stared. She wondered, pulling at her dress, if the plunging neckline was a step too far in what was, after all, a low-key sort of place. It had been a while since she had done this.

'Here we are madam!' The waitress came to a stop at a dimly lit booth at the very back of the venue. She was, Rae noticed, grinning as she indicated the place at the table with a flourish. 'Jesus Christ!'

She had no sooner sat down than she was up on her feet again, recoiling as if from an electric shock. *The hair… The teeth….The ears…*

'I'll be back in a moment with your drinks!' the girl shot over one shoulder and scuttled away.

'Rae! So good to meet you at last. Now I know this will come as something of a surprise but…'

The figure in the corner of the booth moved forward slightly and out of the shadows.

In the light, things did not appear to be much of an improvement.

'Ed? Edward! What the actual… You didn't tell me that you…you're…?' Rae was aware that she was almost shouting now, but could not seem to help herself.

'That I'm Canadian?'

'No! You moron! *You're a fucking werewolf* Ed? Oh Christ you might have mentioned that at some point over the last three months!'

She clutched at her throat. A pair of glassy amber eyes fixed on hers. And what was that? Was he *actually panting*?

A reel unravelled in her brain. Hundreds of messages, late night conversations that ran into the small hours, intimacies shared in whispers, image after carefully curated image sent, little gifts delivered to her work and, worst of all, the *hope, the hope*… All of it was obliterated here and now, face to face with this *monster*. Around them and despite the background music, an obvious hush had fallen as the diners in close proximity

43

concentrated hard on the sawing off of chunks of meat and the spearing of vegetables, their heads bowed over their plates as they strained to catch every word of the drama that was unfolding on table 22.

'I'm sorry! Oh god – I'm so sorry! Look Rae – would you just sit down for a minute and let me explain? Please?' He motioned with a huge paw at the still vacant seat opposite him. 'Hear what I have to say – that's all I ask. Then you can go if you want but – just give me two minutes. Please Rae? Rae-Rae?' *Rae-Rae.*

Her breath caught in her throat. He'd made fun of her name early on in their digital courtship, said that she was too good for something so 'monosyllabic'. So he'd doubled it and she had been 'Rae-Rae' ever since.

'You've got two minutes!" She slid into the booth.
He sighed.

'Look...I was going to cancel tonight when I realised that there was a clash with the lunar... event, but we were getting on *so well and...* After everything you've been through these last few years –'

'Everything I've been through?' Rae banged a tight fist on the table making the candle between them splutter. 'Everything I've been through is precisely *why* you should have told me you were a werewolf Ed!'

'Um...I prefer *lycanthrope* actually if it's alright with you..? Or *wolf-man* even is kinda fun?

Werewolf just sounds so... *Scary* don't you think?'

Rae sat back in her seat. The audacity of the creature! She glanced towards the neighbouring table to see a woman in a velvet choker watching them not in the least bit surreptitiously from behind her menu.

Ed's tufted ears twitched as their server reappeared with a bottle of champagne.

'At least stay for a drink?'

'Ehm..Is this going to be ok for you…sir?' The waitress waived a glass in Ed's direction. His lip curled upwards.

'Did you think I'd need a bowl?' He growled under his breath, 'The glass will be just fine thank you.'

When they were alone again with the two drinks fizzing gently between them, Rae dropped her head into her hands and stared at the table top.

Ed leaned in closer across the table. 'Rae – Honestly? Would you have come to meet me if you'd known? I just wanted to give things a chance. I *really* like you. I was hoping that the feeling was mutual so I decided to just go for it – full disclosure! Remember the guy you dated with the tiny, tiny hands? The dude who was posting your underwear out to random pervs for cash? This can't be as bad as all *that*? Can it? Rae-Rae?'

'Will you keep your voice down! And stop calling me that!'

She looked up and saw that she had hurt him. His expression was… *Hangdog.*

She thought about Rob with the tiny, tiny hands and the day that she had realised she was down to her last pair of bikini-briefs and shuddered… She slid one of the flutes across the table so that it was sitting just below his nose. He sniffed and proceeded to lap at the surface. His tongue, she observed with something verging on interest made a delicate pink scooping motion that delivered the liquid precisely into his mouth.

'How long have you been this way?'

'Oh forever… It's not that bad really. Just one day a month and then it's back to normal. I'm just tired of having to hide all the time. Cancelling things, the lies and excuses, getting caught out at work if I have to do overtime… The involuntary howling… That was a joke by the way Rae. I never do overtime.'

She smiled a very small smile.

'But seriously – it gets exhausting you know?'

'Not really, no.' She held his gaze. Beneath the fur and behind the sharp white teeth, he was in there somewhere.

At table twelve, Annette was listening to the exchange intently. She had not failed to notice those sharp white teeth or the deft pink tongue. Oh the possibilities! Some girls had all the luck she thought as she pushed her now cold linguine round and round on her plate. She could get a lot of mileage out of a little red-riding hood costume with that one – *all the better to eat you with* – for fucks sake! It was just too perfect!

Across from her, Malcolm seethed. It was unnatural for that freak to be out in public like this. To think that only a few years ago they would have been driving 'guys' like him out of town and now here he was, fangs and all, sitting in Malcolm's very own favourite restaurant! He would be having a word with the owner on his way out, or, at the *very* least posting a one star review online as *soon* as they were home. He rolled up his sleeves and flexed his biceps self-consciously. He for one wasn't going to stand for this *woke shite* anymore.

But, as he passed through the restaurant with a stack of plates balanced on his forearm, Marco looked on with approval at the extraordinary couple in the booth at the back. It was incredible how far things had come since his father's life half-lived on the margins of society. He caught one of his servers on the way to the kitchen.

'Make sure they get whatever they want.' He said, indicating with a tilt of his head towards the wolf-man and his date. 'Anything at all on the house ok? And Nino – wipe that bloody cheeky smirk off your face eh?'

Back at table 22, Rae was beginning to relax a little.

'Well, we might as well finish this' she said, topping up their glasses. 'Your tail had better not be *wagging* under there.'

'No tails Rae. That's just one of the many interesting things you've got to learn about guys like me. Don't worry Rae. All in good time. I'll keep you right.' Ed reached across the table slowly. She held out her hand in return and let it sink to the table top under the weight of his paw, surprised by the warmth and the softness of the leathery pads in her palm.

'Let's not get ahead of ourselves here.' She smiled in spite of herself. 'What's it like when it happens?' she asked quietly.

'Annoying mostly. And talk about inconvenient... But sometimes...' Ed's huge eyes locked onto hers, 'Yeah sometimes it's pretty... *wild.*'

#themorningafter
by Melanie Henderson

Commendation, Edinburgh Award for Flash Fiction 2023

Catriona wakes in the grip of a headache, fumbles for Nurofen in the bedside drawer, downs rancid water from a lipstick-stained glass. Her nightshirt is on inside out and she still has on her bra. The underwire cuts into her painfully. She rolls over, sees the empty bottle of Merlot on its side. Oh, shit.

Retrieving her phone from under the covers, she scrolls her Facebook feed.

A picture of her sister, make-up free and glowing, on her way to the gym. #beautifulmorning #upwiththelark #traininggoals.

Catriona swings her legs out of bed, wincing. She keeps scrolling.

A monochrome photo of a colleague and her two smiling sons. #doubletrouble #soblessed.

An old school friend's happy birthday to her husband. #truelove #oneandonly.

There are just two hours before her shift at the care home. The kids are due back from their dad's. The house is a bombsite.

She manages to the kitchen, makes black coffee with three spoons of instant. There is one stale muffin in the bread bin. She puts it on a blue plate, takes a picture. #freshlybaked #fuelfortheday.

She throws the muffin in the bin.

On the way back to bed, she passes her Nike trainers, abandoned in the hall. She slips them on and photographs her feet. #couchto5k.

Likes and hearts start to appear on her posts.

Yawning, she takes off the trainers and crawls back under the duvet.

#winning #lovinglife.

To Protect a Space Inside Which You Can Exist
by Henry Stennett

Editor's Choice, Edinburgh Award for Flash Fiction 2023

So this nextman bounces off me and BANG! slaps against the barbershop window. The growl of the clippers slips. All heads turn. Nextman's record shop tote bag slides down his arm to the pavement. It spills a book—*What White People Can Do Next*—and a poster which springs open to show a hammer and sickle.

He moved to my endz a few months back. Bought the house at the top of auntie's road with his girl. Must've cost a bag. We see dem walking round together, holding white-knuckled hands, preeing wigs and yams. Alicia swears down she saw the girl in a silk durag. No cap.

Thing is, they never look at us. Not properly. They smile—kind of—in our direction, but their eyes look past us. And they take up so much room, bruv, walking six deep with their peoples. Flexing fine-line tats and creps I can't afford. They don't move out of the way or even see me til we're face to face. Streets never felt so narrow.

I hear dem talking bout *how colourful the area is* and *how much further your money goes,* and their friends ask if they don't feel threatened, but they smile bravely and say *it's gotten so much better already.*

Got tired of ducking into the gutter, out of their way. Decided to do something. Blagged this fit from cuz who works at that bubble football place. So, yeah, dem gonna see me now. Feel me?

Seventy-five thousand stitches
by Corrine Leith

Shortlisted, Edinburgh Award for Flash Fiction 2023

I unravel my father's sweater, diminishing the elbow-worn, belly-stretched shape of him until nothing remains but a dozen balls of wool and the scent of sandalwood and single malt whisky.

Variegated shades of blue and grey and deep summer greens creep through my fingers as I cast on sturdy loops of reclaimed wool and misty dawns over dark water, and rainfall in pine forests, and fir cones, and driftwood fires on beaches compressed by stars.

Stitch by imperfect stitch, row by uneven row, my sweater grows, as naive and inconsistent as a child's first joined-up writing. I have not inherited patience, and abandon the pattern to weave my own colours through his muted hues; veins of red and yellow and orange blaze to all points, guided by well-worn threads and an essence biding in an empty chair.

Dropped stitches take me back, un-picking, picking-up, linking-in; securing rescued loops to their neighbours with a click-clack of needles and words whispered from somewhere behind my shoulder, *It's alright, Rosie. Everyone makes mistakes.*

With front and back and arms stitched together my sweater is as vast and shapeless as the space he left behind. I roll up the cuffs, cinch it around my waist with a big-buckled, brown leather belt I found in a drawer and I feel the warmth of him leech from the yarn and seep into my skin. I am armoured now; and ready to joust with the everyday onslaught of life.

Warp and Weft
by Hilary Coyne

Commendation, Edinburgh Short Story Award 2023

It was dark when Corian and I found Andrew Duncan. He was sat on a pile of bin bags at the back of the library, his neck at a squinty angle, eyes blank. A black trail snaked from a sticky lump in his hair. Above him, I made out the dim line of the bridge and the guttering halfway down all bent out of shape. He'd fallen. *Or been pushed.* Corian gave me a look.

We couldn't leave him sitting there on the bins so we dragged him up the side of the building, squeezing through the gap and then past the wall that wasn't a wall – a clever filch of Corian's from the back of the Festival Theatre – and into our square of space. Six feet by six feet and seven stories high. A little lost patch between two buildings that everyone had forgotten about. Our "bit".

I cleaned myself up once and checked the land records. Some idiot had accidentally closed the gap, drawing the two buildings as meeting with only an inch or two to spare. We were off the map, off the record, and free to come and go as we pleased.

I went through the new arrival's pockets. It's just our way. We need to know who's who and what's what down here. I'd learned a long time ago that people, even dead ones, can cause all sorts of trouble so it's best to be careful. That's how we knew his name – Andrew Duncan.

It was too late to do anything with the body so we wrapped Andrew Duncan in an old offcut of carpet that Corian had brought home the day before. Scratchy brown nylon. Institutional. It reminded me of the carpet in the place that we didn't talk about and I wanted shot of it anyway. We shoved the body out into the gap and threw a few bits of cardboard on top of him. We'd have to move him tomorrow but that'd do for now. I pulled the tarp over us and we went to sleep.

In the morning we stepped over Andrew Duncan and went up the road to the Grassmarket. It's important to stick to routines. Corian wandered off down the street looking for useful things so I sat on a low wall opposite Maggie's and scowled at the tourists posing on the gallows spot. Ghouls. Their chattering was doing my head in. I was trying to work out what to do with Andrew Duncan's body but I couldn't think with all that racket. I was about to cross the street when a bin lorry grumbled past and gave me the idea. Now that they'd finally been emptied, we could tip him in the big wheelie bins at the backdoor to the library when it got dark tonight and he'd be off our hands. Sorted.

Later on I headed up Victoria Street. I'd planned to juke up the wee stairs to the Lawnmarket, stay covered just how I like it, but the clock down by Waverley was loud again. It's three minutes fast and it gets right inside my head. Somehow I ended up on the bridge. It was too bright and busy for me but it's against my rules to retrace my steps if I can help it, so I decided I'd go along and slip down by Bobby at the other end.

Past the library I took a wee squint down to the Cowgate below. No sign of our bit. Good. But I felt a strange twist in my stomach as something caught my eye on the stone ledge just the other side of the railings. I reached through and grabbed it then I was up and off along the street before anyone would have noticed, nodding to wee Bobby on his plinth as I passed – attention-seeking, buffed-nose mascot that he is. A few quick steps across Candlemaker Row and I was into the kirkyard and tucked up in my usual spot against the wall to have a look at what I'd found. Just a folded-up piece of old paper. What had I taken that for? Corian trotted into the graveyard then, dragging some frayed lengths of twine. Great minds, well done Corian! We'd use that to tie Andrew Duncan in the carpet before we hoicked him into the bin tonight.

I opened up the yellowed paper and studied it. A cold finger of fear stroked at my neck. Same feeling I get when a door clicks shut or a bell rings. It was some kind of map or plan and straight away I knew the lines of the Cowgate, Victoria Street and the bridge. The library sat at the centre of the plan. What frightened me though was the marking in red pen. A small square drawn over the back edge of the building. An arrow from the Cowgate needled its way in from a question mark in the margin. Our bit.

'Oh, shit, Corian', I said, 'they've found us!'

The bit meant freedom and safety to me. When I was in it I could keep *them* out. Five years we'd been there, Corian and me. Happy years mostly after the years I'd lost. In someone else's bit. Doing as I was told. *For my own safety.*

I stumbled back into the street, panic rising and that demonic tick in my ears. Too much daylight and openness. I needed dark and walls and only a tiny square patch of sky high above to think about.

Reaching the gap that led to the bit, I went to squeeze inside but something wasn't right. The body. Andrew Duncan's body was gone. My heart was banging in my chest and sweat trickling under my arms as I looked at the dummy wall. I moved closer and saw that it was still propped in the groove that held it upright. No-one had touched it. I breathed again and, pulling it back only the tiniest bit, I slid inside and slumped down. Corian wasn't there. He must have run off; he doesn't like it when I get all riled up.

White light pulsed behind my eyelids, a line tracing the loop I'd walked that morning – along and up and over and under. A noose. A weave. Infinity.

#

Woven. That's how I've always thought of this town and its roads and passageways that cross over and under one another like the warp and weft of a plaid. Some lift high on bridges that half the time you don't even notice you're on.

Others dive deep for a while, running ten stories down behind a building that's only five stories on the other side, or push through a closed-over passage, emerging later on to re-join the level above. Those are the ways that I prefer. The low-down, covered routes, the backways and the alleyways, the never-on-display-ways. Beneath the postcards, the tartan tat and the selfies, lives the next layer of the city, grubbier, plainer and crammed with the stuff that accumulates, trapped in the weave. Thread and thrum. All the grime and the unwanted bits winkle their way down here eventually and nestle in the filthy wee crannies of our streets. Like Andrew Duncan. Or me.

When I'm on the move I feel like I'm trailing a thread behind me, adding to the fabric of the city. *Making a contribution.* That's why I have my rule about never going back on myself. You can go past – or under, or over – where you've been but you can't go back and undo it. On bad days, clock days, I walk a lot, pacing the streets around the bit, and sometimes the threads get tangled, and snagged. I notice the ugly, twisted knots later and their existence gnaws away at me but there's nothing to be done. Unravelling is a nightmare and I just make it worse if I try. It's better just to leave the mistakes and try to forget about them.

#

As soon as I woke-up I knew I'd been out cold again. One of those dead sleeps that take me from time to time. I couldn't remember dreaming, just blank, timeless emptiness. Corian was there which made me happy.

I heard a noise outside the bit and I got that shaky feeling in my head. I flapped my hand to Corian and pointed towards the opening. Outside the light had dimmed to the kind of murky twilight that shifts shapes and plays tricks on your eyes. I sensed the change in the sound as someone moved into the half meter wide gap. I held my breath and I could feel Corian's body tensing beside me.

A low voice, 'Eh? I was sure this was where it was. Mebbe need to check from the bridge'. Then the noise of someone stepping back from the gap. Footsteps along the Cowgate.

Corian and I looked at each other. Someone was searching for the bit and they'd been close enough to breathe our air. I was raging. We waited a beat and then slid out past the fake wall and peered round the edge of the building along the Cowgate. A figure was disappearing into the West Bow. We moved out onto the pavement and followed the man as he headed up Victoria Street. I went on up after him, blood rushing in my ears.

The man paused at the top of the street then moved off quickly, turning right along the bridge. Corian and I followed but as soon as we reached the corner I saw he'd stopped at the railing above the Cowgate. He'd taken a yellowish piece of paper out of his pocket and was peering down onto the street below.

'Bastard! He *is* looking for the bit.' Fury hammered inside my head. I couldn't let this happen. Without the bit I'd be out in the open, uncovered. I felt sick. He was up on the stone ledge now to get a better view over the railings, his body leaning right over. Peering. Prying.

The bridge tilted, trying to tip me off, like shaking crumbs into a bin. The red door of the Bedlam yawned its big gob at the end of the road and I felt myself sliding towards it. Bobby must have seen me out the corner of his eye but he kept his gaze steady, fixed down Chambers Street. Wee rat! So, he was in on it too.

My head was thumping with the tick of that bloody ahead-of-itself clock. Its dark bulk and white face were coming right at me now, trying to shove me back. I wasn't having that. Not anymore.

There was a soft whump and the ticking faded. Corian had scarpered so I scuttered on along the bridge trailing my thread. From the way it pulled I knew I'd left a bad knot behind me but there was nothing to be done about that now. I looped back down towards the bit – no greeting for Bobby, treacherous beast. It was properly dark now and Corian was waiting for me, looking at something under the bridge.

The man was sat on a pile of bin bags at the back of the library, his neck at a squinty angle, eyes blank.

Granny's Sofa
by Anne Aitken

Shortlisted, Edinburgh Award for Flash Fiction 2023

Granny lived in her final forever house, which was tiny. So tiny the sofa was also her bed.

The sofa was in a sort of windowed alcove, sunny by day, starlit by night.

The view was marshes and a wildflower meadow where children and dogs played.

The sofa had down cushions and many soft pillows and fluffy blankets the colours of lupins.

It had a heater inside which Granny could turn on in chilly weather.

The sofa could play music and audio books, and waft the scent of lavender and rose geranium.

It could rock gently when required.

Granny was a cranky old, old, old woman.

When they came to take her to a nice nursing home, she pressed a button and the sofa swallowed her up and vaporised her.

Then it turned into a Big Satisfied Smile.

The White Madam's Trash
by Jeannie Armstrong

Shortlisted, Edinburgh Award for Flash Fiction 2023

A new consignment. Aaayeeee! Clambering atop is for the bigger kids. I don't want to risk getting buried under it like my cousin did. He was too ambitious.

Aaaaoooo! The tipper has tipped!

Paper and dust fly around me like evening swifts on the wing. I spit and dribble to emit the dirt. I sleep under that Acacia tree; the one on the right. No one bothers me, except the bad men who come for us and take us away for the night when we don't run fast enough.

My days are spent looking for treasure. When I am bigger I will be the boss wallah. I'll beat the bad men and protect the little runts. I'll beat them and chase them away with a big stick. But now I am going to be the best runt and find enough treasure to eat a big bowl of rice.

Boss wallah! Boss wallah! I found a shiny one!

Our trash pile come across the seas on flat ships. White Madam does not take care of her treasure. I get cut a lot by her broken glass.

One day I will have some sandals like some of the big kids. Until then I must be careful not to stand on glass or metal or get poked by the needles.

I find a picture book with words in it. I hide my book in my clothes to look at later, with my half full belly. Under my Khair tree and my stars.

Waiting for Winston
by Sally Arkinstall

Commendation, Edinburgh Short Story Award 2023

Winston's eyes are closed, he sees so much more that way. His head sinks into the cool cotton comfort of the pillows, his body shrinks between the freshly laundered sheets. Sister Monica smooths his hair beneath her hand, he always was her favourite.

Winston's waiting. He's used to waiting. Today he's waiting, not just for the nurse to bring the drugs, he's waiting for Nelson to bring the news. He tries to count the days since Nelson left. He expects to hear him singing. He listens for his voice bringing life into the whitewashed hospice walls.

He's lucky. He knows he's lucky. He's lucky to be here, where his passing will be blessed by prayers and care from the nursing nuns of the holy order of his education. His mother was right, his schooling did change his life. He wouldn't be here now if he hadn't endured the sufferings of Sister Monica's classroom. He's back in the corrugated shelter, behind a wooden desk. He hears her voice.

'Winston, wake up. Winston, can you hear me?'

'Er, fifty-six,' he guesses, expecting to be wrong.

It takes a moment to pull himself back from the arithmetic lesson. It's not Sister Monica, this is a different sister. He struggles to recall her name. Her touch is gentle on his arm. She lifts his hand, and reminds him where he is.

'Winston, it's Sister Agnes, I have your medication.'

The drug works its welcome way through the cannula and into his veins. He drifts away again. For a while, he's free. Free from pain, free to leave behind the confines of this building and his aging bones.

He's younger now, not old enough for school, still waiting. He's waiting in the dust behind the shacks, hiding in the shade, amongst rows of banana plants growing beside the track. Every day they come now, groups of them raising dust and singing as they rush down the mountain. Huge packs balanced on heads or shoulders, still they run. They're nearly home now, drawn on by hopes of a night with family or friends. They'll hand over their tips, wads of crisp green dollars, then return to the gate to do it all again. Winston wants to run with them, to join in with their Swahili songs. He can't. He knows the songs, but he's smaller than the packs they carry. He waits.

These are the porters. Winston's waiting for the guides that follow. When he sees them coming, he retreats into the foliage. If they see him first, they'll warn the tourists. Winston steps out, unseen, just behind the front guide. He merges into the midst of a group marching down the track.

He holds out his hand. 'Chocolate,' he says. 'Chocolate.'

Today he's lucky, two whole bars of purple wrapped sweetness. It's been carried up the mountain and back again, well wrapped to keep it cool. It sustains the walkers, but they always have so much more than they need. Winston grins for their photographs and grasps the chocolate in his hand. It's getting softer in the heat of the day.

'Snow?' he asks. 'Cold?'

'Yes,' they laugh. 'There's snow at the top. It's cold.'

They turn away as the guides shout at them to keep on walking. The guides have been away for long enough; they don't have time to wait around here.

Winston can't see the mountain's white iced peak from his mother's home, but he sees the snow-capped paintings churned out in the village for tourists to buy. He sees the mountain top from school. Its snowline distracts him as Sister Monica instructs him to write a letter of thanks to his sponsor. He feels her ruler come down across his knuckles. He rubs the back of his hand.

60

'That cannula's bothering him again,' says Sister Agnes. 'I'll get it changed.'

Pain brings his eyes down from the hills and back to the task in hand. He doesn't want to thank his sponsor, he'd rather not be here. He wants to follow his father up the mountain, earn his share of tips. His mother says he must work hard at his lessons. Maybe he can be a teacher, or a doctor, she says. He tells her that he doesn't want to spend his days in school or end them in a hospital.

He's still waiting for Nelson, surely he should be back by now?

'It won't be long now,' he hears. It's Sister Agnes, she's whispering. He knows she's not talking about Nelson.

It's the day the mountain takes his father. Winston's waiting with his mother. She wails when they tell her to wait no more. The priest takes him back to school, finds a sponsor, the one he doesn't want to thank. He's thankful now, or will be when he hears Nelson's voice.

'Winston's a clever lad,' Sister Monica tells his mother. 'But such a dreamer. That boy's head is always in the clouds.'

Winston follows his dreams. He follows them up the mountain and through the clouds. It's his first time. His feet are frozen in his tattered canvas sneakers. He shivers in his flimsy coat. He's not got much to carry, just his own supplies. The porters give him water, two bottles, tell him to drink as he climbs. The water's heavy. Winston pours it away, tells them that he drank it. He's not so clever now. Dehydration and altitude make him sick. Very sick. His meagre tips on that first trip are hard earned, the next time's not so bad.

'Polé, polé, slowly, slowly,' they chant as they walk onwards, upwards, climbing to the camps. They put up tents, take them down, carry them, put them up again before the group arrives.

At first he only goes to base camp, there's plenty of waiting to be done there. The junior porters rest; they sit outside the climbers' tents, guarding their possessions. Winston waits, he's good at waiting.

His feet and hands are cold, always cold. A woman offers him some boots. 'They're old and broken,' she says. 'It'll save me carrying them. I'll replace them when I'm home.'

Winston has never owned anything so wonderful. She gives him woollen socks to pad them out, and another pair for his hands. He stands taller now, loose stones no longer dig into his feet; he doesn't slide and stumble on the path. He bounces as he walks.

'His legs are a little restless, but his feet seem warmer now,' he hears. He feels Sister Agnes's soft hands gently rubbing his ankles beneath the blanket.

It's graduation day. He's fully-fledged, a qualified guide now; he knows all the routes and legislation. He's top of the class, he wins a prize. His mother's face bursts with pride. His son reaches up to him. Winston swings him onto his shoulders and leans down to thank his mother. He must remember to write another letter of thanks to his new sponsors too, she says. He's smiling now, beaming. A wide, white toothed, grin intended only for his mother. They put his picture in the brochure. Winston's joyful face, framed by cloudless blue sky, sells adventures.

'He's dreaming again,' says Sister Agnes. 'Look at his smile.'

Winston's body shrinks a little more each day. His muscles, wasting on unused limbs, grow weaker. Drifts of snow-white hair surround his face as he sinks deeper into the soft mountain of pillows. He spends his days in the edge lands of wakefulness, somewhere on sleep's border. His nights are much the same.

It's Winston's last night in his body. He's back at base camp; it's his first time as a tour group leader. He has his own well-fitting boots now, he thinks he'll hand them on at the end of the season. He doesn't sleep.

'Polé, polé, slowly, slowly,' he says as he guides them upwards, zig-zagging across the frozen scree, towards the unseen summit. Winston sings as he walks, it helps to keep a steady pace. His lungs are used to this thin air, but it doesn't do to rush.

They climb by moonlight before resting at the point; they drink hot chocolate as the sun rises over the plain. Winston talks to the tourists, learns from them, teaches them about his mountain. 'Don't you wish your office was like mine?' he asks as he gestures to the view. Silently, he thanks Sister Monica for teaching him arithmetic and writing. It's his job now to divide the tips, complete the reports. He's always honest, they never find mistakes in his work.

His place, for that final walk along the ridge, is at the back; his job to watch, to reassure and help his group. He takes a picture for them when they make it to the top. Then shouts at them to run, to work with gravity as it pulls them down the scree and back into the richer air.

Sister Agnes hears him shouting, she sits beside his bed.

Back at base camp, Winston sleeps deeply ahead of the long descent. When they reach the lower slopes, he encourages the children who still hide in the plantations. He tells them to wait, to do their lessons first. He shares his chocolate with them.

'I'm grateful for my schooling now,' he says.

Winston sees the business of climbing the mountain grow bigger every year. Celebrities come with camera crews and make-up artists. They even bring a generator for their hairdryers. They make a film to tell the story of receding ice and disappearing snow. Winston's in the film.

'I'm famous now,' he says.

More people come. They want to see the snow and ice before it's gone. They cross the world on planes, arrive at the gates in jeeps. They want to rush up and down, tick the mountain off their list.

'Polé, polé, slowly, slowly,' says Winston.

They want their picture taken with Winston and the snow. They ask him to get on a plane, fly across the world, do a lecture tour. He doesn't go, he can't leave his mountain. He's got a son now too. When Winston's on the mountain the boy waits with his grandmother. Winston won't leave his waiting son.

It's the day his son is born. Winston's on the mountain. He's a senior porter now, still wearing cast-off boots and socks. He's running down the mountain. His mother's waiting. Tears run down her face. She tells him to hurry, the boy's mother is fading. Winston runs but he's too late.

He hears Sister Agnes. 'His breathing's laboured,' she says. 'He seems distressed.'

He seeks solace on his mountain.

'Polé, polé, slowly, slowly,' he tells himself.

'He's calmer now, more settled,' says Sister Agnes.

Sunlight streams into the room. It's Winston's final morning. He knows his time has come. He's still waiting for Nelson. He needs to know the snow's outlived him. In the distance, he hears singing. Not angels yet, not even the chapel choir. It's Nelson. His voice booms and bounces from the silent walls.

Sister Agnes's soft tone quietens the echo.

'You're just in time,' she says. 'He's waiting.'

Winston feels his son's rough skin against his face. He smells sweat and dust. It's mixed with tears and the sweet scent of chocolate, and fresh earth from the mountain's lower slopes. He tries to speak, a single word escapes.

'Snow?' he gasps.

'Yes. Snow. Still there. Still cold,' says Nelson.

Sister Agnes opens a window. Winston feels the warm breeze. It carries Sister Monica's familiar voice into the air-conditioned room. She speaks more gently now, it's only for his ears. 'Your father and mother, and Nelson's mother too, they're waiting,' he hears. 'They've waited long enough. It's time. Time for you to come.'

Winston waits no more. He knows his love for the mountain is safe in Nelson's care. He leaves his well-worn body on the bed. Nelson will return its ashes to the mountain's soil.

Wisdom Tooth
by Jonathan K Bailey

Shortlisted, Edinburgh Award for Flash Fiction 2023

The youngest ever Professor of Entomology was so young that she suffered the pain of a wisdom tooth growing in.

It sat buried in her gum, a firm root that bloomed each day with new and awful agony. It gnawed at her as she worked. She wished for the rough tongue of a cat to rasp the flesh off the bone.

The dentist said she would wait and see.

But waiting didn't get the Professor where she was today. One night, she drank an extra gin, sterilised a scalpel and cut through the swollen gum. The tooth was only just beneath...

But there was too much blood. The gin wore off; she got scared and gave up.

When all the old men had gone home from the lab, she stole a shiny green beetle: native to Turkey, a pest with tiny jaws to pull sugar beet roots from the earth.

She dropped a pipette of syrup and the beetle into her mouth.

It tickled. Then a sharp scratch as it went through the gum. It clasped the tooth in its emerald jaws and pulled. There was a giddy plateau of pain, an unexpected scream, then relief.

Unfortunately the beetle didn't stop there. Its burrowing instincts, and its jaws, were strong. With tiny, rapid bites it dug into her brain.

Police arrested the Professor, on a busy high street, trying to tear a bollard from the concrete.

Her colleagues might have known. She was so, *so* young.

The lost larynx
by Judy Birkbeck

Shortlisted, Edinburgh Award for Flash Fiction 2023

There was a lost larynx, mangled, scarred, in the gutter. Nobody wanted it.

It tried an opera singer, perched on her ear. While the singer let out a burst of coloratura, silver tremolos and silky glissandos, the larynx wheezed and gurgled. The audience wanted their money back.

It tried a Cockney stallholder selling perfume. 'Roll up, roll up, ladies, come and have a look, very good perfume, lubbly jubbly, not five pounds, not two pounds, not one pound, just fifty pence to you ladies.' The ladies walked.

It tried a foetus. Dark and wet, what a racket! Water slopping, thump-thump, thump-thump never ending. When it was born it cried louder than the baby's own. The mother pounced and tore it off.

It tried a herring gull, hollered with the joggling tongue. 'This is good,' it thought. It squawked, meow-ed, keow-ed, it ha-ha-haed. The fish voted with their fins.

It tried an egg, gobbled the chick inside and hatched. The parents chucked it out.

It tried the thunder-god, crash, bang, wallop. It screeched blood. Nobody noticed.

It tried a wave. The surf hissed over the pearly folds and it gurgled with delight. The wave was gone.

It tried a dentist's drill. Like looking in a mirror, like true love. The epiglottis shut it out.

It found a dog's neck with a hole, a perfect fit. It howled for joy. The dog went howl-crazy.

The Fourth Room
by Mary Shovelin

Commendation, Edinburgh Short Story Award 2023

The door clanked shut like a prison gate. Salwa held tight to her husband's hand. She could sense the tension through his fingers. There were too many of them, and shoulders and arms pressed against each other. Salwa thought of the box of dried figs someone had procured for her birthday, each layer tightly packed and stacked neatly on top of the one below. She looked up at the tiny air vents in the roof.

'Will that be enough?' she whispered to Imad.

'Enough?'

'The vents. Are they enough for all of us to breathe?'

'Of course.' He squeezed her hand. 'Don't worry. We've made it this far. This is the easy part.'

She had always trusted his judgement. It was the way she was brought up. Her father always seemed to know better than she did, than her mother did. When to run for the basement, even before they could hear the whistling missiles. When to sit tight at home, clutching their beads. Which shop had bread to sell.

She did not want to dwell on the past. She breathed deeply to calm herself, but she had to grasp the air in mouthfuls. It's psychological, she told herself.

The lorry began moving, slowly at first and then faster. Bodies swayed first one way and then another as it rounded corners.

For a while everyone was quiet. Then low murmurs began. Paper rustled as people started on their meagre rations. She did not feel hungry yet. Her stomach was caught in a vice. We will eat only when we are really hungry, Imad had said. They are supposed to give us food when we stop.

He checked his mobile. The light from the phone lit up his face and she saw dim figures turn towards them.

'You should save the battery,' she whispered.

After a while he shut down the phone and all was dark again.

She wondered where everyone came from. She had checked them out as they were herded onto the lorry, trying not to stare. Someone spoke in her dialect, a woman clutching the hand of a girl of ten or so. They'd exchanged a brief, hooded glance. Others were from further south, and the few words they spoke were foreign to her. There was a group of younger men, possibly in their late teens.

It was a long time before the lorry stopped. Salwa could not tell whether a day and night had passed, or two days. The door opened onto darkness. They swarmed out. It was a motorway service area, empty apart from a few lorries. The driver and the other man shouted at them to hurry, and pointed towards a squat building nearby.

The toilets smelt of bleach and the floor was slippery. Salwa lined up with the other women, waiting her turn impatiently. She had drunk very little of her bottle of water, but now her need to pee was urgent.

As she washed her hands with the trickle of icy water from the tap, the woman and girl appeared at her side. They came from a village near Aleppo, pulverised. 'We're going to Germany, to my cousin.' She nodded at the girl, who stared at Salwa without speaking. Salwa said they were heading to England. She thought of her grandmother pushing her away, saying go, go. Nobody else was left.

'Out!' shouted a man, and she jumped. He banged on all the cubicle doors with the flat of his hand. She hung back a little on the way, searching in the gloom for Imad. The woman and girl were ahead of her. As they climbed back onto the lorry, the driver caught the girl's arm roughly and stared into her face. The mother pulled the girl to her and pushed her ahead. Imad

69

was queuing, talking to another man, and drawing on a cigarette.

She managed to keep a place for him beside her. The lorry started moving before the last few men had taken their places on the floor. One of them fell on someone, and a woman gave a muffled scream. 'Sorry,' he mumbled.

'You were smoking,' she whispered to Imad.

'I got speaking to a guy… We're in Serbia.' This meant that they were not even halfway.

As time wore on, and the mutterings around them turned to snores, her breathing faltered as though a great weight pressed down on her chest. A feeling of dread took hold, and she grasped Imad's arm tightly.

To soothe her, he began to talk in a quiet voice.

'Do you remember the photos Khalid sent us? Their house?'

'The living-room, with the little fireplace?' she replied softly.

'We will have one like that!'

'With a small garden in front, filled with flowers and shrubs.'

'And a bigger one at the back. A bathroom with a shower head that lets the water come down on top of you like rain…'

'And a kitchen with one of those electric cookers, what do you call them?'

'Ceramic, I think. Three or four bedrooms – I'll use one as a study.' Imad was a doctor, and did research to keep up to date. He squeezed her arm and she laid her head against his, and soon fell into a fitful sleep.

Salwa walked through the dwelling they would occupy, and climbed the stairs. They had painted the rooms in pastel shades: green, blue and pink. Their bedroom was the palest of pinks, with a shower room en suite. The spare bedroom was green, with a double bed, ready for visits from Imad's father. She passed Imad's study, packed with books and a sturdy oak desk, and entered the fourth room, where she would study for her final dentistry exams. One booklined wall. A large window looking over the garden. A tall plant welcoming her with shiny outstretched palms.

The jolting awoke her. There was an angry mutter from the other side of the lorry that grew to shouting.

'Stop! Leave me alone!' a woman shouted.

'Water – you have large bottle there.'

'Mine, stop!' the woman was breathless, and there was a sound of scuffling and thumping. A brief scream echoed in the dank air of the lorry, and someone hammered on the wall from the driver's cabin.

Salwa felt for her bottle of water and emptied the remaining drops down her throat. A dry cough racked her chest.

'Got any water?'

Imad didn't answer for a while, and she jerked his arm.

'What's wrong?'

'How did you sleep through that? They were fighting over water. My chest hurts. I can't stop coughing.'

Imad did not speak for a moment. 'Maybe a bug – bound to be bugs going around here.'

When the lorry stopped, a long time later, she got up slowly, her head spinning. 'Fill your bottle,' she whispered, 'in case they don't give us anything.'

'They have to – we paid for food and water,' Imad mumbled.

As people filed out of the lorry, she looked to where the scuffling had been. A woman lay on her side, a stream of blood hardened below her nose. A man pushed roughly past her, muttering 'What you looking at?'

'Off!' shouted one of the men, banging on the lorry with a baton. Imad pulled her along and they dismounted slowly. The chilly air was so fresh that she swallowed it in gulps like icy water. The parking lot was empty apart from a car standing at

71

the other end. A breeze tugged the bare branches of trees this way and that, and Salwa pulled her thin coat tighter around her. The woman and girl were just in front, and both entered the same cubicle together. By the time Salwa emerged and filled her bottle with the trickle of uric-smelling water, the woman and girl were nowhere in sight. It's the toilets I'm smelling, she thought, it'll have to do.

As Salwa mounted the steps into the lorry, a woman wailed in the car park. Everyone turned to look, but one of the men drove them onwards, waving something in the air, which she now saw was a machine gun. A car pulled out, and in its wake the other man gripped the arms of the girl's mother, who was struggling and screaming. As the car passed, Salwa saw the round white face of the little girl in the back seat, eyes huge.

There was a thump and the woman fell silent. She was hoisted into the lorry after everyone else. As she lay on the floor, Salwa made a move towards her. The man held up a warning hand and shouted something, and Imad pulled her back. The door banged shut, and they were on the move again.

Imad leaned against Salwa and took her hand.

'I was thinking, if we have four bedrooms… the children's room should be big enough for two small beds, at least to start with…'

Salwa was silent, shivering.

'What do you think? We could paint it a very bright colour, blue maybe.'

Salwa struggled to regain the snapshot in her head of that fourth bedroom, with its plants and books.

'I'll need it, though, to study, to finish my degree,' she said after a while.

Imad was silent, and she realised that he was asleep. He'd always had that knack of just drifting off, even in the midst of an argument.

She did a 360° turn in her room. Her desk, with a laptop on it. The large glossy plant. The bookcase. Then bunk beds.

72

More bunk beds. The room filled with noise. Children squabbling. A football was kicked and hit her plant, breaking it in two. Salwa sat up straight, coughing.

She could hear a woman weeping and gasping. Her heart tightened.

Feeling nauseous, she swayed in line with the constant movement of the lorry, the swerving, the rapid acceleration into the night. The man on her left did not stiffen as usual as her arm touched his, and Imad lay quiet beside her. Others coughed. She inhaled the dank air. She climbed back into her room, trudging up the staircase, which grew higher and higher, steeper and steeper, until she reached an open door, and all she could see through the dust motes was a mattress flung on the bare floor.

It was hard to tell whether it was day or night, but when the lorry stopped at last, the door was flung open and daylight stole in. Salwa did not want to get up. The two men stood on the threshold, staring. One stepped inside and prodded a slumped man with his gun. Someone moaned. After a fleeting look at each other, the men stepped back out of the lorry and shut the door.

The engine thundered in low gear as though climbing a hill. 'Let us out', someone muttered. Another banged on the driver's cabin. Salwa drifted in and out of sleep. At some point, she realised that the lorry had stopped. She nudged Imad.

'We've stopped,' she whispered. She could just make out his face.

Imad could not rouse himself.

She searched for his water bottle. His hands were ice-cold.

A man lying against the driver's cabin knocked with one fist. 'Let us out.'

'Why aren't we moving?' Her voice was hoarse and did not reach far.

'The bastards…' someone whispered.

Salwa nudged Imad. She turned her face away from the smell from his clothes, but it was no better elsewhere.

She shut her eyes, and climbed the stairs, but they grew steeper again, and her heart battered in her chest as the door to her room receded.

A flock of geese skimmed southwards over the lorry as it stood in the carpark of an abandoned tavern. The sun came and went from behind the clouds, and by the time it set, the knocking in the lorry had stopped, and all was silent.

Barker's Quality Wood Floor Cream
by Barbara Black

Shortlisted, Edinburgh Award for Flash Fiction 2023

Varnish. Top-of-the-line varnish. Master craftsman varnish. Mahogany pianos and cherry wood cabinets varnish. Then the smell of tobacco. Fine tobacco: Louisiana St. James Parish perique tobacco. Drifting in from the sitting room every Sunday evening at exactly ten minutes past seven. Following the smoke, she knew he sat in the Fairington wingback chair. He never spoke, of course. But his presence made the hairs on her arms tingle. She started calling him Vernon and set a slice of pecan pie on the side table before he arrived. He was too polite to eat it. When he departed, there was an indent in the chair seat which lasted a few minutes, then disappeared, just like him. The back door would squeak like a cranky possum, then shut. Rumours haunted the neighbourhood. There was a gentleman caller, but no evidence — except the widow chattering behind drawn curtains every Sabbath. Actually, she wasn't a widow. She was what in polite circles we call a 'spinster'. Despite some girlhood dalliances, love had passed her by. Until now. Despite his lack of corporeality, Violet never loved any man more than Vernon. For the remaining thirteen years, she got on her knees every Sunday at six and cleaned the parlor's maple wood floors with Barker's Quality Wood Floor Cream, then sat down and ate a slice of pecan pie, waiting for Vernon to appear. Tonight, she'd passed away in her chair at 6:59. Still, at seven, the hairs on her arms rose ever so slightly.

No fair
by Michael Callaghan

Shortlisted, Edinburgh Award for Flash Fiction 2023

That's me away Ma.

Ah'm goin' tae the fair wi' Malky and Jimbo.

Whit? How no?

Ah wisnae fightin' wi' Calum!

Ah wisnae! An' anyway, he started it.

He did! He hit me back first.

Naw ah never.

Ah didnae! Ah didnae touch his violin!

How dae ah know? Strings must have broke by themselves.

Calum's always greetin' Ma. Disnae mean it's ma fault.

Ach you're always believin' him Ma. That's shite.

Shite's no swearin' Ma.

Naw it's no! Bastard's swearin'. An' fuck.

Naw Ma! I wasnae actually swearin'! I wis just explainin', that's whit swearin' wis! Aw naw… Ma… dinnae… OWWW!

Whit wis that fur Ma?

There's nae even soap in the toilet Ma. How can ah wash it oot?

Calum does swear Ma. Ye should have heard him yesterday when he never got yon Wordle in the six goes. Shocked ah wis, Ma. Shocked!

Naw — ah'm no daein' the dishes Ma! Ah done them yesterday. It's Calum's turn the night.

He's exhausted from whit studyin' Ma?

He's no a gifted boy that needs rest! He's just a wee sh… silly person.

Ma, ah need tae go to the fair. It's the last night. An' they've got yon new big giant roller coaster. It's bigger than the one Calum boaked his guts up on at Blackpool.

Aw please Ma! Ah'll dae anythin'.

Please Ma…

Please…

Aw Ma that's just shite!

Aw naw… Ma, I jist forgot… Ah didnae mean… Naw Ma, dinnae… please… Ah, fuck it.

Lookin Up
by Jill Fullarton

Commendation, Edinburgh Short Story Award 2023

It wis a hard fecht fur us aw haudin it thegither in thae lockdoons. 'What's your wellbeing tool-kit?' asked the evening paper. Whit the fuck is a wellbeing toolkit? we aw thocht. Hot yoga, kitchen discos, home ballet aw got a mention. Nae way. Ma ticket fur survival? The Edinburgh buses. Ma all-day pass gave me as mony oors gan aroon the capital as a fancied for less than a fiver. Wance a week was aw a could afford. Nae furlough payments fur a brand new trainee chef. A could keep the heid oan a breakfast shift, blowtorch a brulée an chop veg faster than the ithers. Nae use these days. 'Sorry Andy mate, give us a shout when it's all over and I'll see what we can do,' said the heid chef as a packed up ma Sabatiers.

The buses wur deid during the lockdoons. A lot o folk wur feart tae gan oot afore the vaccinations. A always got ma seat o choice on the tap deck richt at the front above the driver. A'd even started taking a wee flask. A'd sip away at ma coffee as we left the Wester Hailes tower blocks ahint. Aff we went past the new skeel. Nae weans the noo. Up the Grange where a could see intae the big gairdens. Folk sittin ootside on posh chairs. Wan lot wi a sweemin pool. Aye, yer haein a laugh in the Baltic city of Edinburgh. Shut theatres that looked fair sad. An the castle. Still the same. Watchin ower the lot o us. Wan time I was oan the bus fur the Thursday clappin. Folk wur hingin oot o tenement windaes bangin pans an clappin like their lives depended oan it. Felt like the bus was gettin a roon o applause as it toured the empty streets.

Noo we wur hurtlin doon the Mound at an awfy rate. No lang an we'd be in Stockbridge where a'd get aff tor a wanner.

A yon cherity shops where stuff costs a bomb would be shut, but if Gregg's hadnae gi'en up the ghost a could stretch tae a pie.

A wis in luck. Gregg's wis sellin their national treasures fae a table at the door. A splashed oot oan a twae fur wan deal an heided doon the path tae the Watter o' Leith. Even noo that we could gan oot for mair than hauf an oor, there wisnae mony folk bravin the killer east wind: only wan dog walker, a couple comin alang aw huddled up thegither. A wis jist a few feet away when a seen it wis Amy. Oh ma god. Amy the receptionist, ma date fur echt weeks an fower days afore she dumped me fur Ben, the maist glaikit tosser kent tae man. A concierge. Aw that have a nice day shit wi the yanks, bookin tables at the Witchereeeee an keeping the tips tae himsell. I slank ahin a bush tae the side o the path, riskin the slippery slope doon tae the watter, but they wouldnae o noticed if a'd jumped oot an flashed at them. If only a'd worked ma way up tae being a chef, captured her hert wi a lobster souffle. Get ower yersell, a thocht as a tanned ma first steak bake.

A bit further alang, a sat doon oan a bench. A pigeon flew ower an landed oan an empty Buckie bottle. Eyeballed me as a tackled ma second pastry. Sometimes a wunnered if we aw came back as birds after we wur deid. A thocht a'd be wan o yon herons a could see fae the flat. Sae tall an jist staunin still at the side o the canal as if they had aw the time in the world. Maw said she'd be a swan, glidin alang tae Falkirk. A thocht she was mair like a blackie. Gallus as hell, aye in the thick o things.

It wis time noo. A took the path up tae the street. Naebody at the stop. When the bus came a nearly let it gan. But the driver had clocked me an hit the breaks, gave him something tae dae a suppose. There wis a wummin sittin upstairs opposite ma favourite seat wi a flooery mask oan. She wis drinkin oot o a jambo watter bottle.

'Awright son?'

79

'Aye, you?'

'Jist oot fur a bit o company, A canny staun being in the hoose on ma ain. It's been months noo.'

'Where are you aff tae?'

'A got oan at Gorgie Road an a'm workin ma way back roon. Lived there a ma married life. A room an kitchen above Ferranti.'

'Handy fur Tynecastle.'

'Oh aye, a loved a hame game. Croods o folk, a richt pairty atmosphere oot oan the street. Me an Davy used tae gan tae the Diggers early an get a seat, stay till it wis time fur the game.'

'A'm an Easter Road man masell.'

"Aye we've aw got oor crosses tae bear. Dae you miss the fitba?'

'A dae aye, Saturdays are no the same onymair.'

'Oor Nicola's talkin aboot gettin it sterted again withoot the fans.'

'Fitba withoot the fans, whae'd a thocht it.'

'An where are you aff tae?'

'Jist ower tae the infirmary.'

'There's nae visiting the noo is there? Is it an appointment you've got?'

'Aye an appointment.'

'A hope it goes weel fur you son.'

'Cheers. That's ma stop noo.'

A few nurses were staunin ootside the main entrance. They wurnae even gabbin, looked fair wabbit. Peely wally ahin their blue masks. I had tae ring a bell, wait fur a while afore a wis let in. A man in the lobby showed me how tae work the haun san machine wi ma fit an a hid tae pit a fresh mask oan. Then a wis shown intae a room wi three chairs aw spaced oot, the windae open, lettin a freezin cauld breeze in. Efter a while, twae wummin came In.

'I'm the patient services manager,' the wan in the suit said. She telt me her name as weel but a canny mind. A wis lookin at ma maw's handbag inside the plastic bag she wis haudin. 'Thanks for coming Mr McLeod.'

'It wis nae problem.' A heard masell say.

'We are so sorry about your mother. And so sorry you couldn't be with her.'

'Wis onybody wi her?'

'I was with her,' the wan in the nurse's uniform said. 'And a medical student who stayed on. Your mum was so well liked on the ward.'

'An she wisnae in ony pain?'

'No, not at all, very peaceful. And she understood why you couldn't be with her.'

Even wi the windae open, A coudnae get ony air. A wanted tae lamp somebody. But it wis naebody's fault. A wis gan tae ask if it would o changed onythin if a'd got her in sooner. A wanted tae phone the ambulance the day afore. Whit's done is done, ma maw wid've said so a jist thanked them, an the wummin in the suit pushed the poly bag ower the table tae me.

'Take as much time as you need,' she said.

It was then a noticed there wis a pair o shoes in the bag as weel. Shiny wans. A remembered maw askin me tae get them while we waited fur the ambulance, slippin them oan tae her feet while she wis lying on the sofa. She didnae want tae gan in her slippers. A jist wanted tae get oot noo. The man at the door gave me a nod an a wis glad tae be away fae the place.

Back on the bus, a put ma heidphones oan an looked oot the windae. A lang queue o folk wis wrapped roon Tescos, keepin their distance an chitterin like onythin. We wur doon the Bridges when a slid ma haun intae the poly bag oan ma knee. You shouldnae look in a wummin's haunbag, especially yer maw's but a took it oot an thocht it ower. As we turned oan tae

81

Princes Street a undid the clip. There wisnae that much really. Two inhalers, haun san, a comb, a reid lippy an a bottle o her favourite perfume. A wisnae up for smellin it. A packet o Silk Cut in the side pocket. Her purse: a opened the bit where you keep the cairds an stuff. A couple o fivers an her library caird stickin oot. An a photae. A slid it oot. There a wis. Ma first day at primary skeel. Short trooser an a brand new haircut. A forced smile on ma wee freckled coupon. A remembered it being taken jist afore the bell rang. Maw giving me a thumbs up, moothing see you at lunchtime as a trailed ower tae the line o weans. Havin maw as a denner lady saved ma bacon. Ma pals loved her. She kent aw their names, made the best puddens, chips oan a Friday. We even finished oor veg fur her. A baked her a cake when a wis ten. A coffee sponge that went aw wrang but she loved it and a wis hooked, sterted making oor tea. Egg an chips, stovies, mince an tatties. When a wis at college, it aw changed an a was oan tae risottos an pavlova. She wis fair pleased. Oot came the camera again fur ma leavin ceremony. When a got a job at the Balmoral she was ower the moon. A clipped the bag shut noo.

The nummer 33 rattled intae Wester Hailes an let me aff at the community centre. A crammed maw's stuff unner ma jaiket and heided hame. The manager o the soup kitchen wis staunin at the door. A kent him fae when ma maw used tae volunteer there. Then a lassie aboot ma age came oot. She wis wearin a pinny, lang dark hair, drap deid gorgeous.

'Everybody's getting fed up with Scotch broth or leek and tattie,' she wis sayin tae him in an accent you could listen tae aw day. 'I mean we're all really grateful to the Co-op for the donations but it'd be great to try something different. Any chance they'd give us some fresh beetroot?'

A knew strecht away whit tae dae. A swaggered ower wi wan o those million dollar feelins that came fae fuck knows where.

'A can make beetroot soup,'

They looked at wan anither, then back at me.

'Borsht. Or French onion. Even Cullen skink, much cheaper tae make than folk think,' a said.

She laughed. In a geid way. A wis oan a roll.

'Whit aboot croutons?' a said.

Noo she pushed a strand o her braw hair ahin her ear an smiled. 'See you tomorrow then, can you be here at 8 am?'

'Nae bother,' a said, an aff a went before the manager could say onythin.

The lift wisnae workin so a bombed up tae the fourteenth flair. Hauled ma crumpled whites fae the back o the wardrobe an grabbed three quid fae the leccy tin. Back ootside, squares o fizzy yella licht were comin oan up and doon the flats. A could see a few stars pushin through the city sky. A picked up ma pace an heided tae the launderette. Things wur lookin up.

Solemates
by Celia Donovan

Shortlisted, Edinburgh Award for Flash Fiction 2023

Sylvie rubbed shimmering, peach scented foot cream into her skin, and wiggled her neatly proportioned toes. She had been complimented on her delicate feet before, with their naturally high arches, but it was only recently that she'd realised how photogenic they were.

Sylvie was an avid online shopper and it was not uncommon for couriers to take photographic proof of delivery. On one such occasion, the burly postman pointed the camera to the parcel at Sylvie's feet and she had joked about including her freshly painted toes. They had laughed and Sylvie caught a cheeky glint in the eye of the man she met daily on her doorstep but never invited over the threshold. Later she noticed that he had indeed zoomed the camera in a little closer than usual.

From there things escalated. The postie captured a series of flattering close-ups as Sylvie worked her way through the colours of the rainbow, from dark mauve with lavender french tips to a playful layer of clear glitter. She donned an alluring toe ring, and ostrich feather boudoir slippers, giving a teasing peepshow of the toes. The more photos she collected, the more she shared on the 'Solemates' foot fetish website. The more money she earned, the more she ordered online; oils and lotions, diamante nail stickers, fishnet pop socks and clear stilettos. The postie never mentioned it, and she acted coy, but she knew from his online user name, 'Toe_Mail_Man' that he was her best customer, and she his.

Things Left On Her Bed
by Michael Forester

Shortlisted, Edinburgh Award for Flash Fiction 2023

Swaddling blanket
Babygrow
Teething ring
Size one shoe
Teddy bear
Copy of *The Very Hungry Caterpillar*
Drawing of Mummy and Daddy
My First Jewellery Kit
Lego brick
Legoland ticket
Cabbage Patch doll
Nail varnish
Toy Story VHS
Copy of *Shout* magazine
Britney Spears poster
Friendship bracelet
Blood stain
Love letter
Bacardi Breezer bottle
Tear stains
London University Students' union card
Spliff
Semen stains
Tear stains
Exam timetable
Engagement ring
Internship offer letter
Smart phone
Wedding dress

MATB1
Maternity dress
Nursing bra
Swaddling blanket
Babygrow
Teething ring
Back to work letter
Tablet computer
MATB1
Maternity dress
Nursing bra
Teething ring
Back to work letter
Love letter
Maintenance agreement
Decree nisi
Furlough letter
Decree absolute
Surgery appointment card
Redundancy notice
CSA letter
Electricity bill
Electricity payment reminder
CSA letter
Debt letter
Breast screening invitation letter
CSA letter
Debt escalation letter
CSA letter
Breast screening postponement letter
Notice of court action
Notice of debt enforcement
Breast screening invitation letter
District Council Children's Services letter
Breast screening postponement letter

Emergency Protection Order
Prozac tablet
Hospital admission letter
Test results
Chemo tablet
Get well soon card
Bible
Hospice admission letter
Get well soon card
Order of Service card

Foraging by Numbers
by Vee Walker

Commendation, Edinburgh Short Story Award 2023

In the lee of a storm-felled oak one chilly autumn evening, there they are, awaiting my knife. Perfect fungi so improbably purple they could have been spored from the pages of *The Thousand and One Nights*.

As I gloat over their silky splendour, my mother enters my head from a different time, another life.

See that sharp break between the cap and the stem, boy?
No ring, no veil.
Break a bit off. Taste it.
Nothing smells as sweet as a wood blewit, eh?
Nothing but you, Mam.

We foraged in all weathers.

Ye're not made of sugar, boy.
Spun pink wisps, melting on my tongue.
Word almost gone now too.

We always took the book we called The Book.

Better safe than sorry…
Mam. Every time!

The Book I kept close by me until…

…not again, boy. Think of other things.
'Other' things? Ha!

Her bedtime tales of scorched deserts, devilish sultans, daring rescues...

...look! Who's this, then? A princess in peril?
Let's see what's in her basket, Mam.

I wait.

The woman approaches from along the track. She hesitates, tucking a thin strand of silver hair back under her headscarf.

The basket seems light, so I speak first. 'Need food, lady?' The seven blewits cover my open palms, slender stems akimbo, fragile violet gills inviting her fingertip.

She comes closer, almost touches one. 'Are they safe?'

Always the same question. I bite back harsher words, for she is skin stretched taut over a frame of bone. 'Oh aye, lady. For sure.'

'Where did...'

I shake my head, look away.

'Sorry.' She falters, falls silent. Then asks instead, 'How many?'

I know fine it's not 'how many blewits' she means by that.

A better question, boy...
...better for me, or for her?

'Two, lady,' I lie.

She staggers, reaches for a sapling. I need this trade as much as she needs to eat, so I spin her a line. 'Found them in a gully. A bit of an overhang. Natural protection, aye?'

'Yes.' I feel her cling to the word protection, like we all used to. She goes to take the blewits but they have already vanished, back into my stiff leather bag. 'Uh-uh. You know how this goes, lady. First, we must trade.'

She blinks once, twice. Her eyelashes are as pale as her skin. Whether from tears, cold or sickness, one grey eye is watering. 'Money?' she asks.

I almost laugh. 'Try again.'

After a pause, she eases one stark shoulder out of the faded shirt, looking round at the bitter ground.

Don't even think about it…
I am not that Other, Mam. Not yet.

'No! Stop! Stop, lady. I only meant something to trade. Exchange. Barter. Aye?'

'Of course. Sorry,' she says again, trying to smile. She has gaps in her teeth, but so do we all.

Act like we're scunnered, boy, and set to move on?
Aye. Usually works.

'No. Please. Wait,' she stutters. 'There's this.' One shaky hand undoes a man's watch.

I take it, listen to it, hand it back. 'Useless, lady. Not a winder.'

She re-buckles its loose futility around her wrist. Her old shoes are split, a dirty toenail poking through one of them.

'I have more things.' She breathes out her defeat. 'At my place.'

'Oh aye? Where's that, then, lady?' She gestures eastwards, up the uninhabited side of the glen.

'Live on your own, do ye?'

> *Could be Others. A trap...*
> ...wheest, Mam. I cannae hear.

'Yes, alone. Now.' She turns. Stumbles away.

> Ach, just look at the state of her...
> *...aye, boy. On ye go.*

She ducks between two rain-contorted beeches, then behind a heap of brushwood, where a narrow path daunders away uphill.

I follow.

Almost invisible, constructed against one side of a wooded ravine, the bothy has large stones at its base: brick, wood, bits of plastic, a tiny UPVC-framed window, even a makeshift greenhouse at the brighter end. A cracked chimneypot puffs faint white smoke, hidden as it disperses by the rocky cleft.

> *Quite a place, eh?*
> Aye, Mam. Impressive.

'Did he die here, then? Your man?'

She nods.

'Where did you bury him?'

She points towards a distant clearing. 'My husband told me to drag him... it... right over there. Our spring is this side, further up...'

> *Clean water runs deep, boy.*
> Once it did. Not any more.

'...I dug. All roots. So hard. Blood. I put stones on top, just like he said.' Wise, now the aban-dogs are breeding back into wolfhood. 'We had a house in a village,' she adds. 'Then Others came...'

> *Oh aye. We know all about Others...*
> ...we do. And what They can take.

'...he found this place. My husband.' She still cannot say his name. 'We camped at first. That dry summer. He kept going back. Wouldn't let me...'

A necessary risk to build all this.

'...will you stay with me here?' Her clammy fingers encircle my wrist.

I shake her off. To forage and sell I must keep moving. 'What have you got for me inside, lady?'

She stoops into the bothy and soon comes out again, a vivid splash of yellow in her hand.

I whistle appreciation. 'Now that, lady… that is worth having.'

The wind-up torch still works. I nod agreement and into her empty basket I drop the seven blewits. She draws them to her, close against her heart.

Seconds later her free hand claps to her face like she has been stung. 'Rain!'

Rain. The dense trees. I have missed the signs, the tarry clouds rolling in from the sea.

'Inside!' she says, yanking me after her.

> I'd never make a cave.
> *No other choice, boy.*

Inside I can just pick out a steel cook-pot set on a trivet over embers.

She takes a rag from the corner, wipes where one or two sticky drops have caught my cheek, then her own. Throws the blistered scrap outside.

> She has done this before, Mam.
> *Aye, with her man.*

The rain has soaked up the last of the daylight. Overhead we hear twigs crackle, sizzle, hiss and fall.

The roof is sound.

She fastens a plastic sheet over the doorway, moves a long sandbag across it.

My belly wheedles. 'What's in that pot, lady?'

'Dried roots. Water. Soon, these.' She gestures to the blewits.

If someone shelters ye from kindness, boy...
...a gift is in order. I know. I know!

'Take this, then.'

She holds it cupped as though I have handed her the moon, then sets my stolen onion on a bit of plank. She fumbles for her knife and I grasp the hilt of my own, but she just chops the onion and slices the blewits. Once in the pot their fragrances meld, masking the less pleasant odours of the bothy.

Who would be daft enough to risk a wash with winter just weeks away?

She adds a little sea-salt from a chipped blue pot.

Pretty thin soup, then...
...give her a chance, Mam!

'Take this.' I pull a twist of dried sea-lettuce mixed with wild garlic from my bag. The woman flinches as I take her hand. I dip one of her slender fingertips into the green powder, mime sucking it. She copies me and her eyes widen. 'Oh! That's good! What is it?'

Perhaps she is younger than I first thought.

'Cook-pot magic. Go ahead, lady. Use it all.' I can afford to be generous. Plenty more drying in one of my caves.

She shows no curiosity towards anything else in my bag, so her next question catches me unawares. 'I go by The Forager,' I mutter in reply. Anonymity is safer.

I do not ask her name, though I can see she badly wants to tell me.

'I will miss that torch,' she says instead, without bitterness. I shrug. A trade is a trade. She has food for tonight, another couple of days, too, if she is frugal.

She stirs the pot. 'Forager?' It seems she has named me anyway.

'What now?'

'Will you test me?'

I usually refuse, claiming my Device requires more sun-charge; but her slender fingers are warmer indoors, their pressure light and desperate. 'Please, Forager. I want to know...'

> ...don't we all, lady?
> Aye. We do.

'Sit still, then.' I run my Device over her head, further away than I should for accuracy, timing each click against my winder.

'Seven!' say the three of us.
Like the blewits, boy. In more ways than one.
Few survive above ten.

'A winter here alone will finish me, anyway.' She says it
with no great sadness, plucking again at her sparse hair.

Nothing more is said until the broth is ready. She hands
me a trembling tin mugful.

I thank her.

A risk, though?
Ach. I'm hungry, Mam. Cold.

This sharing of food softens us a little. She hesitates, then
offers me more.

I decline with a shake of the head: let her think it out of
decency, not self- preservation.

Good thing she didnae ask ye to test her soup, boy…
…ach, give it a rest, will ye!

Outside, the sticky rain continues to scar all it touches.

From curiosity I charge her – my – torch and shine it
around the bothy. Between us another plastic sheet shields a
high ledge of flat stones.

I catch my breath.

Books. Never.
And look, Mam!

Something about the spine of one of them...

...it cannae be, boy...
...it could be, though...

'...give me that!' I make a grab for it but, strengthened by food, the woman blocks me.

'No, Forager.'

'No?'

'No!' Her chin rises and there is a stubborn flash in her eyes. 'To read a book, we must trade.'

'And what if I want to keep it?'

Possess it? Take it? Have it?
Mam! Please. It's The Book!

We both know my last words were a threat, but the woman repeats: 'No, Forager. To read it you must stay with me. For a night and a day.'

'Why should I?'

'Listen. I'll tell you.'

She may be a poor, pale shadow of a Scheherazade, but these rainstorms are unpredictable. We have the time.

I settle back against the wall.

She pulls another branch on to the fire and does not look at me. 'I was... I am... a librarian.'

A library, boy!
I remember now.
Big room, many books, warm, safe.

I try hard not to peer at that one spine.

'The novels went that first winter. The cheap cop thrillers burned brightest. Shiny covers. The heavy classics gave greater warmth. I said sorry to every book we burnt…'

The sound I make at that might be sympathy or scorn.

'…I did! At first. There were so many.'

She points to the stone shelf, ignoring my expression. 'These are the last, you see. He used them. To build all this. To feed us.'

A good man. Like you.
Once, Mam. Even then, only maybe.

'Reference Copies Only,' she says fiercely, brittle arms hugging her knees.

I point at the spine I covet. 'OK. Let's trade, lady.'

She kneels, slides it down and out from the plastic, places it in my lap with both hands, her head bowed.

I stroke the cover. Its familiar heft tightens my throat. 'I never thought…'

'…so, Forager. You'll stay?' It is a confirmation, not a question.

'Yes, lady. I'll stay.'

She sleeps before I do, curled under a blanket of badly-knitted blue and purple squares. Her hand, upturned and outstretched, suggests that I could join her there.

Instead I wind the torch to awaken The Book. The first spell it yields makes my blood sing. This night I will dream of a cruel and cunning birdlime, crushed from holly and mistletoe. Dream of how we shall feast on a fat, clean, roasted woodpigeon...

> *...and will you not dream of a snare*
> *set by a thin librarian, too, boy?*
> Right enough, Mam.
> Aye. Right enough.

The Back Road and the Kissing Gate
by Rosaleen Lynch

Shortlisted, Edinburgh Award for Flash Fiction 2023

We walk the back road, barefoot on the middle strip of grass, holding hands, long shadows of our summer skirts swishing with our steps until the kissing gate, where you let me go into the far field of my family's farmland and you say you'll see me tomorrow, not knowing it will be a lie, that I wouldn't rush to supper if I knew, that I'd have held your hand longer, or told you that you'd grown over an inch that summer and I could prove it, and I'd have asked you if my lips were bruised purple with blackberry, like yours, and warned you about the nuns, that the only thing they hate more than girls kissing boys is girls kissing other girls, and I'd pack my suitcase and run after you instead of waiting for you next morning at the kissing gate, and I wouldn't go late to school and ask about your empty seat and have to hear the teacher say your parents sent you away to a convent up the country, and I wouldn't wait for a letter from you, or for spring to come before I leave the farm by the far field gate, finding the v-shape in the fence, following the hinged arm round, to let it close behind me, to take the back road alone, and I wouldn't have to wonder every day where you are and if the convent they have you in, has a back road and a kissing gate.

God Save the Queen
by Ann MacLaren

Shortlisted, Edinburgh Award for Flash Fiction 2023

It's a two mile slog to the nearest Jubilee party, but the girls are used to walking and Stella knows she can jolly them along with promises.

'There'll be cakes,' she tells them now, 'and chocolate biscuits. But you'll have to eat sandwiches first. At least two.'

With any luck they'll eat more than that before they start on the sugary stuff.

Rosie waves a paper she made at school; it's torn at the edge, and the straw holding it is grubby now. She and Nina are wearing red T-shirts and blue leggings. Stella has a red, white and blue headband holding back her hair; she's no unionist, or royalist but she doesn't mind becoming one, just for the day.

As they reach the gardens they hear squealing and chattering and teacups rattling. A colourful clown blocks their way at the gates, but he only wants to offer the girls a balloon.

A woman with a posh, commanding voice herds them towards a table with vacant spaces. Another woman smiles and passes along a plate of food. Stella eats her sandwiches graciously as she chats to the families around her; she's just moved in to the neighbourhood, she tells them. They're too polite to ask which street, which number.

Nina and Rosie quietly eat their fill; later they all watch the entertainment while Stella, unseen, slips tomorrow's dinner, one by one, into her large handbag.

'The Queen,' someone calls.

'God save the Queen,' says Stella, gathering up her girls.

Faerie Food
by Lily Laycock

Longlisted, Edinburgh Short Story Award 2023

The faerie came in the evening. As I sat in my garden, spread amongst the grasses, I smelt her. The raw, stinging scent of cut flowers.

I looked up to see a woman of the forest with hair the colour of ground cardamom. Lingering where the tamed garden met the undergrowth. With a curl of her fingers, she stepped back into the darkened tree line. Her smile was carved, a dark imprint on her face as she retreated. My body keened forward, drawn by her smell, on the trees, on the heather. I dragged white skirts through mud and bracken, all to follow her. The sweet-smelling woman.

The forest which I had known since infancy was twisted into strange paths. Paths which curled and folded over like waves, spilling toward the woman in front of me. I fell and crawled; my fingers crunched leaves and I held them tenderly to my face, smelling the brush of her foot sole. Skin, sweat, a loose strand of hair. I followed them like a breadcrumb trail, chancing glances up to make sure I did not lose sight of her. When she finally stopped in a clearing, I could see her for what she was.

At first I thought she was bleeding. The naked arches of her shoulder blades were broken down the centre, the inner linings of her skin drawn out and draped flaccidly down her back. But as the forest pulled in tighter around us, so her form grew. Dozens of jittering insect wings spilled from her body, spread out like folding glass windows. Her face was split into fractals behind them as she turned back and smiled. A smile which ate up her face and split into soft, pink layers. The petals of an unfurled dahlia, her gums and teeth, gaping back at me.

I stumbled onto my knees and edged forward. As I went, I disturbed toadstools in the soil, ripping their fat round bodies from root.

The faerie crouched down and I extended my hand to her face. Touched that mouth and traced the rows of her petal lips. Her breath, so sweet that I could drink it like sugar water. I swallowed the scent, letting it fill my nose and throat. I embraced her in my dirty arms, the linens of my clothes stained with the forest floor.

She held me, wings beating fast and heavy, nails pincers in my back. I had seen body-snatching wasps in my garden penetrate a caterpillar's fleshy hide until they were filled with dormant eggs. Larvae that ate the contents of the body and bore tunnels to the surface. In a fouled white dress draped in the arms of this intricate creature, I prepared for her sting. Her fingers in my mouth, running the rims of my teeth and opening my jaw wide. I tasted her with a sharpness I had not yet known on my human tongue. The sour note of citrus. Before it turned sweet, so sweet that I trembled with salivation.

She fed me from her fingers and mouth. Allowing me to bite and tear at the petals on her face. Ripping them free and tasting a flesh that shamed all fruit and flower. I ate and swallowed until I was ripe with nectar. It swelled in my stomach and spilled back into my mouth.

Falling from her arms and to the ground, I vomited the excess. Dry, sharp stems forced their way up my throat and I pulled them out. Cutting my fingers on my teeth, I withdrew a sprig of lavender from my lips. Slick and yellowed with saliva.

The faerie laughed.

When the sun rose over the forest canopy, I awoke alone. I licked my lips and sniffed the air before I began to weep bitterly in mourning. The faerie was gone. For her smell, no trace of it remained.

I pulled up the ring of mushrooms that surrounded me in that patch of forest, piling them within my skirt. When the ground was plucked bare, I began to wander back the way I came. The route was marked by crushed grass, flowers, and fungi. I cradled the mushrooms and made sure not to drop a single one.

Once home, I cooked and ate them. Though I could feel their texture and presence in my mouth, their flavour was absent. Not spoiled or bad, but completely dislocated.

I spat out the rest and washed away the muck in the sink. Pieces of grit and dirt fanned out amongst the water and coloured it grey. I hadn't tasted any of it. My tongue searched my teeth and found a brief sweetness. I pulled a damp wing from my mouth, iridescent and segmented like a fly. Though I searched through the sink, I could not find its body.

Bread was flavourless, too. Milk and cheese, even when left to curdle. Fish, laid out in the sun to salt and dry. The absence of taste turned my body thin as I did not eat. The insects that died in the window sills of my home wet my mouth but turned my stomach. Sinful temptations, roasted in the sun until their legs curled and their eyes burst.

That night, I knelt in the garden and stared towards the tree line, waiting for her to emerge from the forest. My faerie, who had fed me so well. Her flesh, which tasted like no other meat. To which no bruised fruit in my garden could compare.

Evening left the sky and I was still alone amongst the flower beds. With no moon, the world was flat grey and leeched. I lay down amongst the flowers and pulled them over me, blanketing my neck and chest. As I squeezed a handful of lavender, I heard a muffled crunch. Heat rose in my palm, followed by dull pain. I uncurled my fingers to see a wasp. It had been tucked inside a lavender stalk. Now, its brutally yellow body emptied the last of its venom into me. An angry goodbye as it died in my hand.

Brushing its remains on the dirt, I lay back in the lavender and spread my arms. The heady smells rose around me: lavender, lady's mantle, violet. I opened my mouth and fed on the aroma. Another insect crawled across my cheek but I ignored it, even as its stinger pricked under my eye.

A sting which turned into a finger against my skin. Scraping down and to my mouth, where it gently wormed inside. Blissful sweetness and warmth, the taste of metal that became sugar in my throat. I opened my eyes and found my faerie, her body pressing mine into the flowerbed. She smiled and pushed a sprig of lavender past my lips.

I ate it whole. She fed me another. They melted to oil and leaf in my throat, leaving me choking for air. She continued to slide them in, filling me with flowers. My tongue delighted at the taste, starved for so long. The petals, the stems, the insects, churned to ambrosia inside my mouth.

When the faerie leaned in to kiss me, I was no longer breathing. She pushed me down into the earth, past the beds of ruined petals and soil. There, she clung to me like roots, worming her way around my shell. Until we were deep within the dirt.

I stayed buried beneath the garden for years, until my bones became cavities for the flowers above. The garden flourished, feeding off my body and hers. The faerie and I, made one. She lay with me, our forms collapsing together.

She was peaceful, contented. Her duty carried out, she was free to sleep for the rest of her days. And I, to feed the flowers.

The Number 22 to Ninewells
by Paul McFadyen

Shortlisted, Edinburgh Award for Flash Fiction 2023

15:03 *This stop is Peddie Street, Peddie Street*
A greying lady takes one look and gets up, presenting her palm to the vacant space as she smiles at my belly. I didn't think I was showing. The firmness I feel faces forward. They say that means it's a boy.

15:07 This stop is Kelso Steps, Kelso Steps
The houses here watch water between its slopes to Fife. You can see the stumps of the rail disaster. Big, stone houses filled with big, stony morals and proverbs about responsibility, no doubt. If I had one of those to come home to, would I have made the appointment? If I had one of these to come home to, would I have needed the appointment?

15:10 This stop is Elliot Road, Elliot Road
I told him that if he meets me at the hospital, then we can talk. He can't lecture me then keep fucking off when push comes to shove.
A man sits near, smelling of beer and I retch.

15:12 This stop is Dochart Terrace, Dochart Terrace
Gran's wee flat was just over there, looking over Dickson Avenue. It's by a primary school and church. You can still see the water, but only just.

15:15 This stop is Spey Drive, Spey Drive
Maybe we'd end up living here and I feel myself grimace at the idea.

15:17 This stop is Ninewells Hospital where this service terminates

I wait until the bus empties before I alight, searching for his baby face.

The Power of Social Media
by Stuart Murray

Shortlisted, Edinburgh Award for Flash Fiction 2023

Pet_Lover_79	Has anyone seen our cat? He's been missing for 2 days. His name is Banjo.
Metal _Guru	What does he look like?
Pet_Lover_79	I have attached a picture below.
GandalfsWand	That's one fat cat!
Pet_Lover_79	Banjo has a glandular problem. He needs a special diet.
FrodosFeet	Mince pies and chocolate cake?
LostPa55word	I saw a cat like that on Tuesday.
GandalfsWand	Outside a cake shop?
Pet_Lover_79	Banjo went missing on Thursday.
LostPa55word	I was on my way home from the dentst. I had an absess.
Pedant20406	Dentist. Abscess.
LostPa55word	???
Pet_Lover_79	Has anyone seen Banjo since THursday?
GandalfsWand	If I had seena cat that fat, I would not have forgotten that.
AlisonWonderland	i saw a real fat caat yesterday outside carpet world
AlisonWonderland	it was not as big aas the one in that pic
AlisonWonderland	aand it was ginger and not black and white
Patrick1995	Are you certain that is a cat? It looks fartoobig to be acat,
DebbieDevon	My daughter wants a kitten. Any 4 sale?
GandalfsWand	Don't buy a kitten now. Feline-Godzilla might eat it.
Wendy&Barry	Stop fat shaming the cat!!! She has a medical problem!!!

Wendy&Barry	How would you like if we talked about your car like that???
GandalfsWand	If my car was that big, I wouldn't be able to afford the petrol.
FrodosFeet	Looks like it swallowed a boa constrictor already!
Pet_Lover_79	Sorry. I attached the wrong picture.
Pet_Lover_79	That's a photo of Baskerville, our Afghan Hound.
Pet_Lover_79	Banjo is now safely home. Thanks everyone.

Bright Lights
by Avis Wakelin

Longlisted, Edinburgh Short Story Award 2023

You set off along the road in the thickening twilight. You know this pavement well, every stone, because your feet have trodden this route for the last seventeen years. Aged three, you could fit six tiny steps into one of these stones. Now, you cover it in one easy stride.

Six streetlamps serve this road on the edge of town; they're widely spaced and pools of darkness lie between each one. As a young child you'd break from your mum's hand and race through the terrifying dark to cling to the next lamppost, giggling at your small triumph.

You've reached streetlamp one. There's no-one else here, only you. But you're used to that. This small northern town has had the life sucked from it. You've felt its creeping despondence for years. The coalmines closed before your time, all physical traces quickly smoothed over by public parks and bright new builds, like an embarrassing relative who has to be hidden from public view. But the legacy of those days is kept alive by the old folks here. You see them through the window of the last remaining pub, huddled over their pints in rheumy reminiscence of earlier times, before they succumb to mournful graves. Throughout your childhood you watched the shops close, one by one, saw the arrival of charity shops and discount stores and as you grew you felt the comforting certainties of young childhood peeled away. Now the blank eyes of boarded-up shopfronts confront you as you walk down the high street to collect your mum's bits and pieces. In your fractured community the young wreaked havoc: theft, wanton destruction, addiction, the usual litany of bored youth, before they left for brighter lights and big cities, with empty pockets and high expectations. But not you.

Streetlamp two, and along the road all six lamps flicker on, hesitant, as if reluctant to illuminate a lost cause. You can clearly see where that paving stone sticks out proud of the others, its edge forced up by the roots of the ash tree in the garden of number five, and you tripped over it once in the dark when you were ten. Did it hurt? You can't remember now, because pain has no memory. And even at ten you had the sense, maybe in your mother's protracted silences, your father's deepening moroseness, that your world was changing. Out of fear you stuffed your mum's silences with idle prattle, regaled your dad with silly jokes. You thought you could make a difference, but she didn't talk and he didn't smile. You failed. Is this where it started, the slow unravelling of belief that the world held you in its hand?

Here's streetlamp three. Your dad's moroseness turned to violence and your mum filled her silences with vodka. For the first time in your life, at twelve, you felt profoundly afraid and your future was a gaping void of irresolution. You started bunking off school and failing in your subjects. At the counselling sessions they sent you to, a tired woman shuffled bits of paper and kept getting you to close your eyes and imagine a happy holiday scene. She looked how you felt. At home your dad walloped you for getting poor exam results. Out on the streets, life with your new mates was safer, fun. You took your cue from them and rolled your skirt up your thighs, applied your shop-lifted eye makeup in the bathroom of Alice's house while her mum and dad worked nights. You were brash, sassy, high on new possibilities, sealed tight into your own brittle and impregnable certainties.

You've got to streetlamp four. Your high heels ring on the empty pavement and already they're hurting your feet. You lean against the post and ease them off, wiggle your cramped toes. You wonder why you chose to wear such unfamiliar footwear, all you ever wear is trainers, but you have a feeling, though you can't be sure, that this isn't a trainer situation and you need to make the right impression. You pull the shoes back on, smooth your hair.

Streetlamp five. You're going to meet Joe, or maybe Jo – you've only spoken to him on the phone. But Jed's given him the thumbs-up and you like Jed, you trust him. Jed knows a thing or two about life: he's lived in London and he's twenty-three. There's a small horizontal mark scraped on this lamppost, about three feet high. Your mum made it when you were about seven, measuring over the top of your head with her nail file. You can still hear the rasping noise it made. There, she said, you'll be able to look at this when you're big and tall, and she laughed. You push thoughts of your mum out of your mind.

And so to streetlamp six and your footsteps are slowing. Your dad cleared off, who knows where? Thank the Lord, said your mum and things improved. She cut back on the vodka and you got a handful of GCSEs. You want to study graphic design. Your friends left and it was in the balance but you stayed. Then your mum brought Tim home and she went all fluttery eyelashes and tight tops. You don't like Tim; you don't like the way he looks at you, the way he trails his hand across your bum when he walks behind you. You don't like what Tim might do to you.

Just past streetlamp six you turn left, up Coronation Terrace, slower along Connaught Street and left again into a cul-de-sac that you've never noticed before. And here's the door. It's shut and the curtains are pulled tight. But this is the door, you're sure of it; number nineteen. It's glossy green with a brass knocker shaped like a horseshoe and your eyes bore into it as if willing it to yield the answer your question. Tomorrow, if all goes well, you could be on the coach to London. For a moment you let your mind embellish the sketchy image you've permitted yourself of your future: a little flat, maybe in Camden Town or Chelsea, at work in an airy office with skylight windows, discussing the finer points of some design. You got an A for Art in GCSE and Joe said you have the right potential for Marketing; but anyway, you checked out the name of the company that Joe has connections with – you're no fool – and it seems good. And yet...

Raspberry Ripple
by Liam Nolan

Shortlisted, Edinburgh Award for Flash Fiction 2023

It was love at first sight for Leroy. He'd felt like this before of course, almost too many times to count, but somehow this one managed to eclipse all that had come before her. Even though a sweltering bank holiday had brought a sweating mass of sunseekers down to the seaside, she stood out from everyone else, a beacon in a shimmering sea. Her curves, her sweet ruby-red folds running through her like crimson lightning, the way she glistened in the sun. It was all too much for him. Even though he knew it was wrong, he had to make his move, otherwise he would regret it for the rest of his life. He swooped down, snatching his love away, sound-tracked by a child's heartbroken wailing. An indifferent attendant tapped the sign reading 'No refunds if stolen by a seagull' and went back to scooping more ice cream for the long line of holidaymakers. Leroy landed his conquest back to his perch, cracking open her delicate cone and losing himself in her cool, sweet softness. *It was true*, he thought, as he sated his hunger. *Forbidden love truly does taste the sweetest.*

When Sunflowers Weep
by Toyo Odetunde

Shortlisted, Edinburgh Award for Flash Fiction 2023

He is positively gorgeous. He's filled out since they took him from me. His face is appetisingly plump now, bursting with ripeness. Baby oil irradiates his deep complexion, giving him the satisfyingly glossy sheen of polished mahogany. She's buttoned him into a smart butter-yellow pinafore. An excellent choice, contrasting against his skin beautifully – delightfully reminiscent of a sunflower.

I watch them surreptitiously from the same secluded corner at the back of the café as I always do. He gurgles and gobbles and dribbles and belches and throws out his dumpy limbs from the wooden highchair spasmodically. He giggles admiringly at her, and I am pleased. Relief swirls inside of me, warm and comforting like brown liquor.

I stifle the agonising urge to run to him, to feel the plush smoothness of his face against my palms as I gently massage the fleshy abundance of his cheeks. Sweet relief is quickly eroded by bitter despair.

He continues to fidget and fuss and kick, and knocks over a small tumbler. It shatters, pieces of orange juice-stained glass leaping away from one another dramatically. He shrieks, exhilarated by the sight and sound of the commotion he has created. I cannot help but smile. I decide that he has inherited my mischievousness, and my anguish is assuaged by the knowledge that despite our separation, there will always be something of me inside of him.

She slaps him.

A torrent of stunned silence inundates the café.

I begin to weep. And so does he.

Pushing up Potatoes
by Gina Fegan

Longlisted, Edinburgh Short Story Award 2023

Mrs Murphy sighed as she looked out the window onto her scraggy back garden, the grass was patchy, a few hardy daffodils were in flower, the rest of the garden showed the signs of a 'one time vegetable plot' now run to seed. Deep in thought she considered that her first early potatoes were chitting in the cupboard under the stairs, with the eyes already showing shoots. She'd gone for Maris Piper's this time. Rockets were fine but as she didn't know when she'd get them into the ground had decided Maris Piper was a better bet.

Ruminating, she was not sure if she was sad or angry, this should be Jim's job. She was only coming to terms with the fact that he wasn't ever going to do the potatoes again, and he'd been dead nine years already. This spring was worse that ever. She was completely on her own, she'd hoped that their son would be back in time to take over the garden, but that wasn't going to happen.

She sighed again, deeper. Letting the net curtain fall back into place she turned, went back down to the kitchen, and switched on the kettle for a cup of tea. As the water was boiling, she rooted through her box of 'bits 'n' bobs' identifying the only pen that worked and took down a packet of reduced price Christmas cards.

All of her movements were slow and painful. Arthritis, or general ageing, showed that digging the garden was not a realistic option.

Taking out the card with the snow scene, which she hoped wasn't too 'Christmassy', she began:

'John-Joe, you are the best of sons. Whatever they say, I know you didn't do it. Anyway I am looking out the window and thinking there's no hope you will get parole before St Patrick's Day to be able to do the garden, so I will ask Mrs Gorman's son Thomas to come round and dig the back for me. He's a strapping lad and could do with a few bob. Unless you know of anyone else? I love you, and I know you could never, ever, hurt a fly. Looking forward to my next visit, your loving mother, Ita. xxx'

The 'xxx' curled around the edge of the card due to the lack of space. She kissed it before slipping it into the envelope, looking sadly at the prison address.

A few days later Ita Murphy was looking out the front window, surprised to see the postman with a letter in his hand that was clearly not a bill nor some marketing flyer. She popped the kettle on before she opened the door.

'A cup of tea Pader? I see you have something for me. And I have a packet of Marietta opened and sure they don't last long before going soft, so you may as well help yourself.'

The postman didn't say anything but slipped into his usual seat at the kitchen table as he handed over the mail. Everyone knew that Mrs Murphy's son was in jail, no-one believed he could have killed anyone, tax-fraud maybe, but murder? No way.

Tea served with milk and sugar, biscuits on the table, she opened the letter. As soon as she had seen the writing, she knew it was from John-Joe.

'Maam, STOP! Don't let Tommie Gorman do any digging around in the back garden! That's where the body is buried! Your loving son, John-Joe xxx'

She nearly dropped the letter. She didn't, but it was lowered just enough for the postman to see what was written.

'I'd best get going now' was all he said, thinking he'd dine out on this gossip for a week at least.

Still clutching the letter, she followed the postman down the short corridor to the front door.

As they opened the door, the postman stepped back in surprise and knocked into Mrs Murphy. Before she had fully righted herself, she could see why he'd walked into her.

There was a crowd swarming up the path towards the front door. A crowd of policemen, policewomen, crime scene tape, cars with flashing lights and someone was erecting what looked like a gazebo for summertime sun lounging.

The postman managed to slip through the melee but not before he heard the first policeman say, 'We have reason to believe that there may be evidence of a crime buried in the grounds of this premises...'

It didn't need the postman to spread the word. All the neighbours were in the street in groups of two's or three's swapping the little information they had, and adding a great deal of speculation. Those who had first floor windows were sent upstairs for a good look and messages were sent down to provide as much of a running commentary as possible.

Mrs Murphy's house was in a terrace. Like her neighbours on either side, it had a gate with the space for one car to drive in and park, an ornamental hedge separating the car from a front garden for flowers and a sad patch of grass on either side of the concrete footpath leading to the entrance. The back garden was about twice the size. All in all, not very big. So the police kept most of their equipment on the pavement, now cordoned off with the special 'crime scene' tape. The uniformed police were standing around while their colleagues covered themselves in their 'hazmat' suits.

Mrs Murphy was to stay in the house. Regaining her composure, she made more tea and asked about all that special clothing getting dirty. 'Call me Ita' she said to the special branch officers as she refilled their cups. And in response they made sure that the muddy footwear didn't traipse through the house but used the lane that provided a back entrance into the rear garden.

By midday the news cameras arrived. The whole street was full now. Vans, cars, press and news reporters. 'Would they find a body?' was the question that each of the neighbours answered in turn. Mrs Murphy could see the gossip and wanted to come out and defend her son, but she was kept inside, just in case she was needed.

By the end of the day she was almost out of tea. All the Marietta, and anything else she had in the kitchen, had been eaten. The work was slowing down.

It was still early spring, so the sun had gone down and frost was creeping in before the policemen called it a day with nothing to show for all their hard work yet.

Mrs Murphy climbed the stairs to look out the window and by the light cast from the open curtains she could see the damage. Every square inch of earth had been attacked, dug, examined, poked, sieved and abandoned. There were a few bits of debris, a Starbucks cup from the coffee drinkers, a fluttering bit of tape left from separating the areas already dug, from those yet to be dug.

A few days later, she was still drinking her first cup of tea when the postman appeared.

This was unusual.

He had another letter for her. She poured him a cup from the pot and set it out in his usual place before opening the door.

'Morning Pader. No biscuits this morning, they've eaten me out of house and home and I am not to go out yet' she said as she let him in.

He approached her with his arm outstretched, the hand writing on the letter clearly visible. It was another one from John-Joe.

No wonder, Pader had rushed round with this one. Everyone wanted to know what was going to happen next.

Mrs Murphy, looked over her glasses at him, said nothing, and carried on drinking her tea. She would open this one on her own.

Closing the door behind the postman, she looked at the letter again and smiled.

Slowly and carefully she slid a knife under the flap at the back of the envelope. With a sharp brutal action slit it open.

'Dear Maam, it was the best I could do. You should be able to get the potatoes in the ground in time for St. Patrick's Day. Your loving son, John-Joe xxx'

She smiled again. John-Joe was a good lad. He'd never hurt a fly, unless she told him to.

Gut Instincts
by Cecilia Rose

Longlisted, Edinburgh Short Story Award 2023

Ah've always gone wi' ma guts. Ma gut instincts. Ah just know things. That's how ah operate. But havin' said that, ah still didnae see how this whole thing would work oot.

'Are you accusin' me of stealin'?'

That's how I spoke tae hur, even if she was ma boss, cos ah was black affronted. I was practically splutterin'! Inside ma heid ah says – count tae ten, hen, and ah manages tae keep ma temper while Alice grits hur teeth and carries straight oan.

'I already explained to you Helen. I'm not accusing anyone. I'm just giving you the facts. Money has been disappearing from my mother's purse. Jewellery has disappeared from my mother's dressing table.'

Alice has got me in the kitchen and she's keeping her voice low even though her ma's deaf as anythin'.

'Well ma conscience is clear,' ah says, 'If a wis gontae take anythin', would ah hiv waited for two years? Cos that's how long ah've worked for you.'

Alice looks aw sorry for herself then and she apologises.

'Listen,' ah says tae hur. 'Its no me. Ah would niver take anythin' from anybody. I can assure you.'

'I know, Helen,' she says, 'But I'm telling each person as their employer that this is what has been happening. And that if it doesn't stop – then I'm going to the police.'

I takes a good look at hur. She's very tired lookin' if truth be told – in hur forties, thin face, hair dyed jet black which doesnae really suit hur, although she's got an expensive jacket and skirt on for hur work.

'Listen Helen,' she says, 'I can't ignore this. There's a diamond bracelet gone missing. It was my great-grandmother's and its worth thousands!'

'Aye, ah mind that, bracelet,' ah says. 'Your Mum showed it to me, and she took it oot hur jewellery box!'

'When was this? Have you seen it recently?'

'Naw. That was the week ah started. And that's the only time I ever saw it. Maisie said she didnae wear it cos the safety catch was broke. So the wee bit stuff she does wear is always oan the top tray. Ah thought it was still under there.'

'So did I,' she says, and her voice is aw stressed. 'My brother was the one who actually noticed it was missing on Friday. He was checking through all her things for insurance purposes. So then I had to tell him that I had noticed other things, small amounts from her purse, bits of jewellery , over the last few months. But I hadn't said anything to anyone, and Gerald was really furious.'

'How come you didnae tell anyone?' ah says.

She sits doon at the kitchen table.

'I hoped I was mistaken. I hoped... oh I don't know what I hoped... I just didn't want to have to deal with it.'

'Right well,' ah says, 'Ah'll deal wi' it the now. It's no me. It's definitely no Norah. It's no Aileen either, it canny be. And it's no Agnes. Unless... is there anybody else wi the chance tae look through your mother's things when we're no aroond?'

She had her heid in her hands, at this point.

'There's no one else. You know how careful I am.'

'Right. Well. The rest o' us jist wouldnae steal – Ah'll swear that on ma life.'

She looked at me, and it was a strange look, and she goes,

'I wish I could be as sure as you are about things, Helen. How can you be so sure?'

'Cos a trust ma guts,' ah says. 'Ah trust ma gut feelin's.'

Her eyes filled wi tears and then ah really did feel sorry for hur, cos she's tryin' tae run her ain business, wi two teenagers tae see to, and an ex that disnae want tae know aboot them as far as ah can make oot. On top o that, hur muther's got dementia plus she's runnin' a private team o' carers so her ma can stay in her ain hame.

I was goin' tae offer tae make hur a cup of tea but then hur phone rang frae hur work, and she had tae go.

I went up tae the bedroom tae look in on Maisie but she was still fast asleep – in front of Talkin' Pictures. That's what she likes. She used tae be able tae follow the stories and talk aboot them, but noo she jist likes tae nap through them, efter hur breakfast, and then she's fine for goin oot later. She's an affy nice woman. Nae bother. Jist cannae look after herself any mair.

Ah couldnae sleep that night for thinkin' aboot the whole thing and ah thought, 'There's nothin' for it, Helen. You'll jist have tae become Mrs Bloody Marple and solve this.' Cos ah already knew who had taken the bracelet – ma guts were telling me. I just had tae prove it somehow.

So next mornin' – it was ma mornin' aff – I phoned roond the lot o' them, Norah, Aileen and Agnes. They were aw ragin', same as me, and Norah jumped at the chance tae come roon tae mine, tae hiv a coffee.

She arrives wi Tunnocks Teacakes and the whole thing worked oot.

'It's got to be Alice herself,' says Norah. I heard that she's got business worries. 'Maybe she took the bracelet and the brother's noticed its gone and asked her about it. So she then says there's other stuff gone missing. Maybe nothing's really gone missing *except* the bracelet! We've only got hur word for it.'

Ah could see Norah really liked this idea. She helped herself tae another Tunnocks tea cake.

'Naw,' ah says, 'It's no hur. Don't get me wrang – she's quite a tough cookie in hur ain way – but I cannae see hur stealin her ma's diamond bracelet and sellin' it, no matter what.'

Nora shrugged at me.

'So?'

'It's the brother'

'The brother?'

Aye! Its him! He's planned it! Stolen some other wee things furst, then takes the bracelet, and then goes tae his sister and starts accusin' us!

'But you've never even met the brother,' says Norah.

'Aye ah have. The once. At Christmas. And ah didnae take tae him.'

And ah helped maself tae a tea cake cos ah suddenly knew it was dead simple.

I phoned Alice and ah told hur tae come over tae the hoose again on Sunday mornin' cos ah had an idea aboot who it was. I knew I could get Maisie fed and showered and parked in front o' the telly again and that would clear me a wee while tae chat.

She arrives aboot half an hoor late lookin' awffy harassed.

'Right Alice,' ah says, 'Check oot yur brother.'

'What?'

'Check him oot! He's the one noticed the bracelet had gone missin'. Hiv you thought that he might hiv took it, and aw the other stuff, tae cover himsel' so he could put the blame oan us?'

Noo it was hur turn tae be black affronted.

She goes pale and she says, 'But Gerald would never...' And then she stops, and I could see her eyes change.

'Wait a moment" she says, "Gerald..'

I keep ma mouth shut.

'Helen,' she says eventually. 'I think you might be right. There are things he's been telling me that, well, that don't always make sense. I'm going to look into something...'

And she gets up and she goes – just like that.

And ah thought, Bingo! She knows somethin'. And then ah felt sorry fur her again, cos a dodgy brother is the last thing she needs when she's losin' hur mother mair and mair every day.

A week goes by and she phones me tae say she's coming over tae her mother's at the same time, so ah does the same routine again, and its aw fine, and ahm waitin' for hur in the kitchen wi the kettle boiled.

She looks pale as anything but she gies me a wee sad smile.

'You were right,' she says, once we were sittin' doon at the table. Gerald *was* up to no good. I've been to see my lawyer. It's all very horrible, but if he's sensible, he won't make me go to the police.'

'So he admitted takin' the bracelet?'

'No. He completely denied it! Got very angry with me and said it must be one of you. He even suggested it was me! But the way he behaved made me angry enough to go to the bank and get access to my mother's accounts. We both have Power of Attorney but he has always managed her finances and just given me what I need to pay all of you.'

She takes a deep breath.

'He had set up a direct debit to his own account from my mother's savings! He was just helping himself! He's been paying himself six hundred a month for the past year and a half! When I challenged him, he admitted it. He said it was money that was coming to him anyway when mum dies. Can you believe that? And then he accused me of taking the bracelet again. Called me a hypocrite!'

Ah wis actually stumped for something tae say, apart frae – whit a bastard.

Instead ah says, 'Dae you want a wee cup o' tea, hen?'

And she just sat there and gret her eyes oot.

'The thing is,' she says, after she had got a cup o' tea doon hur, 'If I'm really honest, I did know about Gerald. I felt there was something not right when he got his new car. But I pushed it away.'

'Aye,' ah says. That's yur gut. Everybody knows everything deep doon. That's whit ah believe.'

And she says, 'Thanks Helen.'

And ah says, 'Don't mention it. And dinnae worry aboot me telling the others aboot this. Ma lips are sealed.'

As she was goin' oot the door she says tae me. 'The only thing I don't understand is why he won't admit he took the bracelet.'

So she went back tae hur work and ah sat doon tae think aboot that, cos it was botherin' me as well.

And then ah knew the one thing none of us had thought o' dain'.

I went up the stairs and Maisie's in her wheelchair in front o' the telly watchin' Bette Davis.

Ah chats a wee bit and then ah says, 'I remember you showed me your grandmother's diamond bracelet. Do you know where it is?'

Ah didnae want tae upset hur but ah had tae see what she said.

'Is it not in the jewellery box?'

I got the box and showed hur it wasnae there.

'Its worth a lot of money.' she says. 'I would hate to lose it.'

'So you don't know where it is?'

She shakes her head and she looks upset and ahm thinkin' how tae distract hur, but she suddenly looks up and smiles.

'It's in the bank,' she says. 'I put it in the bank.'

She points tae the cupboard, and when ah open it, there's the big piggy bank someone gave her for her birthday marked Granny's Pound Pot. Ah turns it upside doon and the bottom comes off dead easy. And inside is a heap of pound coins, a few bits and bobs of jewellery, and the diamond bracelet.

'I had a feeling' she says. 'I don't want Gerald to take it. I put it safe for Alice when I'm gone,' she says. 'It's for Alice, not Gerald.'

I learned three things from it aw.

First, ma guts point me in the right direction but they're no a hundred percent accurate.

Second, ah quite enjoyed dain' ma Miss Marple, and ah' would dae it again if I get half a chance.

Third, no tae get too carried away wi masel'. Turns oot, dementia or no dementia, ah wasnae the only one wi' gut instincts.

Silent Resistance
by Andy Raffan

Shortlisted, Edinburgh Award for Flash Fiction 2023

In the morning they will come for me. They will call it justice. I killed two of their soldiers. In fact, indirectly, I killed many more. When they've taken your husband and son, what choice is there? Mine was to be silent. Silent in the sullen food queues, watching and not watching. Counting how many soldiers. Number and type of vehicles. What weapons were carried.

Silent as I passed through checkpoints, face unreactive. Translating and storing deep their words – where they were going, when, for how long. Silent when I fished the scribbled notes from my underwear in the rubble-strewn alleys and pressed them into faceless hands.

Silent when I found the soldiers in the cellar, standing over my daughter. Smells of alcohol and old metal. A pistol in my hand, warm and slick like a tumour. Then explosions. Once! Twice! And she was in my arms, sobbing, as I dragged her upwards and outwards, through the house, filling a bag with clothes and tins and pressing crumpled notes into her soft hands and whispering in her ear 'Go, run, don't stop, don't look back, Mummy loves you always,' and watching her stumble into the burnt-out street, wishing and not wishing she would look back for one last glimpse of her face before the night took her.

I see shards of daylight. They will come soon. But I will be silent. They will get nothing from me. I raise the pistol and for an instant there is thunder.

It Comes in Waves
by Kelly Railton

Shortlisted, Edinburgh Award for Flash Fiction 2023

As his wife talks he eats poached eggs on toast, takes an occasional drink of his coffee. He hears only the rolling of the sea as it retreats from the beachfront café.

Out of the corner of his eye he can see her gesturing hands, her coral t-shirt. Occasionally she stops for a quick sip of tea. Then she talks again and words he can't quite catch meet with the shushing of the waves.

The waitress clears away the dishes and he smiles and nods, pushes his empty plate towards her. His wife, usually the one better with people, has nothing to say.

They had spent so many happy, loud summers here. They'd sat in these same seats, keeping an eye on the kids as they built structures in the sand. At first tumble down pillars, and later full castles, with moats and fortresses.

The waitress returns with the bill, places it carefully in front of him. He unfolds it and sees they have undercharged again. As he explains the waitress twists and untwists her cloth.

'That's right, sir. Remember?'

She bends down, avoids eye contact and says more quietly, 'Remember? It's always just one coffee and breakfast now…'

He notices his wife is still silent, closes his eyes, takes a deep breath.

'I'm sorry, it must be so hard.'

He opens his eyes slowly and nods. The waitress takes his payment and he turns his face to the sea, away from the empty chair.

'We are now arriving at our final destination. Please make sure you take all your personal baggage with you'
by Mandy Wheeler

Longlisted, Edinburgh Short Story Award 2023

A phone rings. A phone is answered.

'Hello. You've come through to the Lost Property Office, Poultry Department.'

'I beg your pardon?'

'Sorry sir, just a little joke. You've come through to the Personal Baggage Department. Did you leave something on the train?'

'Oh, right. Yes, I did. I was on the 19.20 into Paddington and I, um… Look, I'm sorry, I don't know how this works.'

'Don't worry, sir. If you could just give me a general description of what you've lost, then we'll have an idea of where to look. What kind of personal baggage are we talking about? Envy, resentment, low self-esteem? Transgressive relationships? Morbid fantasies? Fear of commitment?'

'Well, I'm not sure how… '

'Confusion it is, sir? Life lost its meaning? You're overwhelmed by the thought of your insignificance in the enormity of the universe? Powerless in the face of your own mortality? Or is it a phobia sir? Cats, clowns, cheese?'

'No, I— cheese??'

'You'd be surprised, sir.'

'I'm sorry, I'm finding all this rather embarrassing.'

'Ah. Sexual, then. Performance or perversions? Or is appearance?'

'Appearance?'

'Is it your looks sir? Height? Weight? Put on a bit recently, have we? Or is it, you know, 'other dimensions'? If so, I'll pass you over to Geoff. He looks after body image issues. Very big department that one. Hair's in there too if that's your worry. Too much, too little, wrong colour, ill-advised comb over...'

'No, it's...interpersonal.'

'Ok, I see. Family baggage. Repressed or acting out?'

'I'm not repressed!'

'In denial then. We keep the Unacknowledged Truths in the basement. Mother related or father? Sibling, half sibling, sibling you never knew you had, mother you thought was your sister, father you thought was your uncle?'

'Stop it! It's not my family.'

'Ah, anger issues, we—'

'I'm not angry! I'm lonely. Well, I was lonely. That's why I'm calling. I've lost my loneliness.'

'Oh, well why didn't you say, sir? We've a huge loneliness department.'

'You do?'

'Oh yes. Bit too big, frankly. We can hardly keep on top of all the stuff coming in. People talk on trains, you see. They get chatting to a stranger, make a connection, then forget to take their loneliness with them when they leave.'

'Yes. That's it, that's exactly what happened to me. There was this nice-looking chap sitting opposite. I noticed he was reading a Graham Greene. 'The Quiet American', the Penguin Twentieth Century Classics edition. I'm a great Graham Greene fan. So, we got talking and then, as we left the train, it turned out we were both going to the Underground. So, we took the escalator together and at the bottom, he turned left to the Northern Line and I—'

'I think we've got the picture sir. So, you had a nice chat...'

We did. But then when I got home...

'Something didn't feel right.'

'Exactly.'

'You were missing the eggs?'

'The eggs?'

'Man goes to the doctor and says: 'You got to help me, doctor, my brother thinks he's a chicken.' Doctor says, 'Well, why don't you bring him in?' Man says, 'I would, but we need the eggs.'

'Oh dear. Do you think I'm very stupid?'

'Like I said, it's not just you, sir. Loneliness is a big department. Poor old Maureen, she hasn't got time to catalogue it all. That's why we ask you to come in and look through it for yourself. Fridays, six thirty to eight, we open the department.'

'Six thirty to eight?'

'Yes, though often it runs a lot later. Turns into a bit of a party, you see. Sociable lot, the lonely. Only, a word to the wise—if you're needing to pick up any paranoia, perhaps leave that till afterwards. We nearly had a nasty incident last week when someone missed out on the Pino Grigio.'

'Right. Ok. Well, I'll see you on Friday then. And, er, do you think that, maybe…?'

'You might meet the man from the train? Exactly what I was thinking, sir. It often happens like that.'

'And if…?'

'And if you do, we'll be happy to hang on to your loneliness for a bit longer, don't you worry, sir. There will be a small fee of course.'

'Of course.'

'So, we'll see you Friday then. Goodbye sir—and good luck.'

For a Time, I
by Hannah Retallick

Shortlisted, Edinburgh Award for Flash Fiction 2023

Washed his coloureds and whites separately; hung them neatly to dry on the makeshift line that I'd fashioned between the garden fences; peered distractedly out of the window because they said it wouldn't rain but you can never trust them can you; hurried out with the round-cage washing basket; unclipped his pants, shirts, trousers; huddled over them when the pitter-patter started; scurried back into the house with his mound of spring-dried clothes; folded them into neat squares or hung them in our wardrobe that smelled like Pledge; tidied my lips into red and my tiny body into a crisp white frock, the one he said he liked that time; didn't worry about why he was chronically late or that he got so cross if I asked; used the extra minutes to prepare a story about my day that had nothing to do with washing his coloureds and whites separately because that would not have interested him in the slightest; couldn't imagine there ever being an occasion when I might throw them all in together, neglect to use fabric softener or even detergent, switch the temperature to ninety degrees centigrade, watch through the machine's door, listen to the gurgle as the mangled clothes turn painfully, and wonder what might happen next.

A Glimmer of Long-necked Hope
by Taria Karillion

Shortlisted, Edinburgh Award for Flash Fiction 2023

Carim's earliest memories of Aleppo were the bone-shaking cart rides with the warmth of a wide-eyed calf on his lap, laughter-filled hours playing with the other traders' children and the fathers haggling and philosophising over bubbling narghiles with their writhing wisps of smoke. But his *favourite* memories were the secret messages with Uri, month by month, in miniature scrolls of hand written happiness, hidden in the stable's mousehole in a tiny, long-necked bottle.

But that was years ago, in a world where clean and well-fed were normal, and sleeping with one eye open was not. Much, if not all, had changed since then; except his aching core of hope. That remained; burning bright, warming his thoughts like hot, mint tea on a winter's night.

Nevertheless, it was surreal, to now, finally, stand in the rubble of the once vibrant market square, stirring its mourning veil of dust and ash, still daring to clutch a shred of expectation. Would it still be there? That last message, never collected; the address of Uri's Aunt to whom they'd fled when the fighting drove everyone out.

In the jagged remains of the stables, Carim crouched in what was left of the very last stall. Slowing his breathing, he felt an unfamiliar stretch across his face as that tiny bud of hope began to swell into a bloom of trembling warmth within him. There, in the mousehole, barely visible among the tangle of debris, was the smallest glint of brass — a tiny, long-necked bottle.

Skates
by Aidan Semmens

Longlisted, Edinburgh Short Story Award 2023

It was the first big freeze of the year and all week talk in the cheder behind the teacher's back had been of whether the river was frozen deeply enough for skating. Now it was time to find out. Even the boys who had not been studying all week, but working were out on the ice – the tinsmith's son, the boys who helped their fathers with the glassmaking or woodworking, the boy who hawked his mother's fresh-baked bagels round the streets.

Isaac had new skates, a gift from his grandfather. They fixed to his boots with leather straps and metal buckles and had solid, silvery blades half an inch deep. All the other boys wore flat wooden skates they or their fathers had made, tied to their feet with string, a single length of wire wrapped around from front to back and stretched tight to provide an edge. On some feet they worked much better than the shop-bought skates of which Isaac felt not proud, as he knew he should, but secretly rather ashamed. Some of the boys openly admired them, but he envied them their hand-hewn blocks of riverbank willow. The skates, his better boots and his newer clothes were all symbols of the difference he felt between himself and those around him. His long black gaberdine seemed to him less suited to skating than the thick bundles of hessian and rough brown cloth the other boys were swaddled in. In cheder it came easily to him to debate more smartly than others. He was proud of his successes in learning, his regular prizes for cunning argument, whether in Torah, Talmud or the newer subjects, science, mathematics or Russian. But he knew he would be prouder if he had to work harder to achieve them. At skating he lacked the co-ordination, the bravery and bravado that made a fast or stylish mover. He knew that if he were to try harder he would get better, but never enough to be among the best, so it made for lesser disappointment if he were to try less hard. He suspected much the same might apply to the most dedicated and proficient skaters when it came time to return to the candlelit gloom of the classroom.

Still, he had to admit to himself that skating could be fun if only he could really let himself go. There were moments when he did that and he soon found that like the others around him he was panting clouds of steamy vapour into the chill air and could feel his face breaking into a smile.

'Hey, look at Gurvitch!' someone yelled and there was a burst of laughter shared by a few young voices.

Isaac did not know what he had done that was funny, but he grinned as if sharing the joke and was glad that every face was red anyway so the embarrassed flush he could feel in his cheeks would not be apparent.

Then he felt himself swept up in a group of boys he knew only by sight. A rough hand was on his back, another gripping his sleeve. Whether they were pulling him along, whirling him around among them, in simple friendliness or for some other motive he could not tell.

He grinned with them and tried to stay upright on the ice. When, inevitably, he fell, arms reached down to help him up. It was all right. Everyone fell over from time to time. No one would notice or care if he fell less gracefully than others. Again he fell, and again. He would have bruises. But he was having fun, wasn't he? This was what it was like to have fun. Then a conspiratorial arm was around him. The boy's unpleasant breath was in his face, the voice low.

'Do you sleep in the same bed as your sister?'

The honest answer would have been 'no'. Isaac felt that the answer wanted – what might have been the true answer if another boy had been asked – was 'yes'. That was what he said.

'Bet she feels nice under the covers,' said the boy. 'Can you feel her titties yet?'

'She's only eight!' Isaac exclaimed.

'But she's pretty,' said the boy.

'Well, she would be,' jeered another, 'if her eyes didn't look two different ways.'

Then suddenly the boys took off at speed in a frenzy of laughter and only now did Isaac notice he had been led out onto the exposed ice of the river. It was lighter here, away from the overhanging trees, but also colder as curling patterns of blown snow scurried around his feet. He could skate back to join the boys he knew, now beyond sight or hearing around the curve of the stream, but he did not want to follow those who had just left him here and in any case he wanted to compose himself before being seen by his classmates. After a few moments in which the cold seemed to close in on him, he began to slither his way upstream into less familiar territory. He could sense, rather than see, the tall bulk of the Christian cathedral looming somewhere above him.

As he approached the Arsenal bridge a harsh voice arrested him, yelling something in coarse Lithuanian, a language he struggled to understand.

'Hey, Jewboy!'

He knew that much. Should he ignore it and carry on the way he was going?

Should he turn back? He was still undecided when they caught him under the bridge.

The stonework was grimy in the deep shadow of the roadway above, the road that led out of the world he knew into the bigger, strange world of the Christians. One large icicle dangled over his head.

There were only three assailants, but they were older and bigger than his previous tormentors, perhaps fourteen or fifteen. They were as expensively dressed as he was, though in smocks and knee-breeches and sporting flat caps with shiny black peaks, pushed back jauntily, quite unlike his own round fur hat.

'What you doing here, Jewboy?' said one, taking him by the upper arms while the other two slid round behind him. The boy had the beginnings of a dark moustache on his fat upper lip.

Isaac was more confused than scared. Though these boys were strangers to him, he knew that his father worked mostly for the better-off Lithuanian families, probably for the fathers of these very boys. He tried to stand as straight and tall as he could, though they still towered over him. He tried to say something calm and dignified. It came out in Russian. Then his skates were kicked out from under him and he fell much more heavily than before, hurting his back and his elbows as they struck the hard ice. For a moment he shut his eyes and at once he could feel the heavy bodies on top of him, their knees pressing him down, their hands invasive. His hat was pulled from his head, a handful of his own gaberdine forced into his mouth, preventing him from yelling. He was affronted, angry, even as he gasped for breath and struggled to free himself. And then he felt cold ice against his suddenly bared buttocks and a tremor of fear rushed through him with the cold.

Limping home slowly without his skates, Isaac was afraid his parents would punish him for their loss. They did not. But he was unable to respond fully to his mother's repeated inquiry about what had become of them, and for that his father spoke severely to him and sent him early to bed, where eventually he cried himself to sleep. 'If you won't explain to us, perhaps you will explain to your grandfather who bought them for you,' said his father. 'In any case, there will be no more skates and no more skating.' And for that, at least, Isaac was not sorry.

'So, man-kin,' said Adolphus Gurvitch, 'they tell me you lost your new skates already.'

Isaac stood with hands by his sides and looked at the floor of the dark, heavily furnished, book-lined apartment.

'Yes, grandfather,' he said. All day he had been dreading this moment, sure the old man would fly into a rage, or worse be downcast with disappointment. So far the gentle voice betrayed neither of those emotions.

'So how? How were they lost?'

Isaac stared at the faded geometry of the ancient rug.

'You didn't like them?'

'Yes, grandfather.'

'Yes you didn't like them, or yes you did?'

'I liked them, grandfather. Thank you.'

Adolphus, dwarfed by the high winged back of his favourite armchair, sat facing the boy at a distance of a few feet across his half-dark study. He waved away the thanks as if shooing a fly.

'You liked them but you lost them. The first day you wore them. Careless – but the loss is your own. Now again you have no skates.'

Isaac examined the worn, turned-up toes of his grandfather's leather slippers.

Adolphus turned to Isaac's father, who stood almost filling the doorway, his arms folded across his chest.

'The loss, however it occurred, is the boy's own, Aaron,' he said. 'I doubt there is anything you or I may do about it now. It happens. I also doubt that he mislaid them anywhere or allowed them to slip from his feet to the bottom of a frozen river. Either he gave them away as an act of charity, even though he liked them' – he turned his head to give Isaac a significant look – 'in which case, he is a good Jewish boy. Or he lost them because someone took them and he failed to defend his property with his person. In which case…' He cast another, longer look over Isaac, who continued to stand with his gaze half lowered. 'In which case, he is a normal Jewish boy.'

At this Aaron uncrossed his arms and batted at the inside of the doorframe with the back of his hand. 'If that is what it means to be a normal Jewish boy, I'd rather he didn't grow up Jewish,' he exclaimed.

'Feh,' said Adolphus. 'Always with you some reason to abandon your people. If you had stuck to your Talmud... You were a good boy for your Talmud.'

'If you had stuck to your Talmud, father, instead of learning law, we would not be in this house now. You would be muttering your prayers at this moment in some cold synagogue, not here in Vilna but in some godforsaken shtetl. You'd be dressed in rags, living in a hovel – and you wouldn't have money to waste on skates for an ungrateful boy to lose.'

'Isaac is not ungrateful, are you Isaac?'

Still without looking up, Isaac shook his head. At this moment he did not trust his voice.

'So,' continued Adolphus. 'Perhaps the shtetl would not be such a bad place to be. I would not have to suffer the arrogance of a son who makes a living helping wealthy gentiles get wealthier. Gentiles, I might add, who consider your brains and learning merely as commodities to be bought, inferior to their vulgar money. I would not have to see my grandson robbed by vulgar goys, too timid to fight back or even to tell his own family the truth.' Once more he turned towards the boy. 'That is what happened, man-kin, isn't it?'

At last Isaac raised his head. His could feel that his eyes were swollen, his cheeks red and tear-streaked. He nodded.

Marta Schneider can't say Goodbye
by Katherine Powlett

Shortlisted, Edinburgh Award for Flash Fiction 2023

Only one adult permitted to accompany the child to
Westbanhof station.

Only one. Not Pappi and me together, waving and
smiling, encouragement planted on our lips to conceal the tears
behind our eyes.

**The number tag, issued during the luggage inspection,
must be hung around the child's neck with the allocated
number, written in black, facing outwards.**

My musical mathematician. My son. My only love. Not a
number.

'You're going on an adventure. On a train. To England,' I
say, afraid the staccato pounding at my ribs will betray me.

Excitement keeps you awake.

'Pappi and I will join you when we get our papers,' I
promise.

Sweat breaks out on my creased forehead. My heart folds.

**It is forbidden to pack documents, drinks, jewellery of
any kind (especially gold and silver), valuables, and money,
except 1 Reichsmark for drinks while in transit.**

My hands are vibrating like a string on a violin as I fumble
to pack the regulation case.

My wedding ring, sewn into the corduroy collar of your
wool coat.

A photograph of us standing proudly before our shop. But
now the windows are in pieces, the walls daubed JUDE.

An ivory hairbrush, my hair woven in it.

A handkerchief soaked with a perfume of tears, marked
with a drop of my blood.

All the love I can give, hiding in plain sight for you to uncover when the truth crescendos inside you.

Accompanying adults must refrain from waving and speaking loudly.

Refrain? I can't. Pappi will say the last goodbye.

Auntie Dragon
by Frances Gapper

Longlisted, Edinburgh Award for Flash Fiction 2023

My aunt's door no longer shuts properly, because of the rubbish. As we navigate her hallway, stepping over dusty piles, she fires questions at me. 'Still unmarried? Good. No children? Wunderbar. Run your own business? Kerpow!'

According to a social worker who peered through the window, hoarding is an illness common to lonely old women. The neighbours tilt their heads and say 'ah, poor thing.' I don't believe my aunt is either lonely or pitiful. But I can see the storage issues have become a problem.

She flourishes a wrought iron key, unlocks a corner cupboard. Inside: a chipped eggcup, a pile of tatty children's books. Young and old heads of Queen Victoria on worn dark pennies. 'You'll have these', she promises, 'after I'm gone. In another two hundred years.'

My aunt burps a gassy flame. 'Whoops, pardon me.' She covers her mouth with a scaly paw.

Peacock Shit
by Michael Boxall

Longlisted, Edinburgh Award for Flash Fiction 2023

Nature abhors a vacuum and things imagined seep into the memory to fill the gaps left by things forgotten. That might account for my memory of the peacock.

It stole Mum's bra so we chased it through the park and down the Champs Elysee with a spatula. Passers-by threw rice until Hemingway came by to lend us his Mauser and we cornered it in an abandoned hamburger joint down by the river.

Imagination, obviously.

So how did that peacock shit get on my shoes?

Superpower
by Gillian Webster

Longlisted, Edinburgh Short Story Award 2023

We walk side-by-side on the boggy ground. It rained overnight and the pavements are slick with downed leaf litter. My daughter's hand feels small and warm in mine, her fingers sticky in that child-like way that is more endearing than gross. My mind is on the slippery path, the speeding traffic, the day ahead. Lucy's head is in the clouds, as always.

She skips as we near the corner, breaking free to press the button on the crossing light. WAIT! The word illuminates on her command, and she drifts back to my side, pleased with herself.

'Daddy. *Dad!*' She tugs on my sleeve as we scamper across the road.

'Mm?' I say, distracted as I guide us around a pothole that is deep enough to swallow Lucy's shoes and ankles.

'What's your superpower, daddy?' Her tone is that of a grown-up who's unhappy at being ignored.

'My superpower?' I repeat the question, buying time to come up with something that will satisfy my curious girl.

The slippery pavement becomes a steep Edinburgh hill. Cars flee past, their tyres spitting dirty water in our direction. I use our joined hands to guide Lucy closer to the wall. The road feels like a racetrack missing a safety barrier. Understeer, oversteer, one moment of inattention, a car, the wall, and us. It's terrifying.

Oblivious to my fears, Lucy decides I need help with my answer. This is her go-to when she senses I'm not paying attention. She offers examples, as though I've failed to understand the question instead of the truth, which is that I've allowed my adult worries to crowd her hopeful little voice out of my head.

'*So,*' she says, with a loud sigh. 'Mummy's superpower is hugs. Her hugs make everything better. Like when you took my game away last week because I wouldn't share with Ethan. Her hugs are *magic.*'

'I've noticed that,' I say, because it's true. My wife's hugs are the best. They're warm and generous, all-encompassing in the way she folds her arms around you like she is a receiving blanket, and you are a newborn child.

'Martha said her mummy's superpower is getting the last parking space at the supermarket,' Lucy says. 'I asked Arthur and he said his dad can make a plane take-off by going for a wee.'

She giggles after she confesses this. I find myself grinning, too.

'Know any more people with superpowers?' I ask, warming to the idea.

'Aunt Elaine said she can magic up a table in a restaurant even when it's full.'

I can believe this, although I keep it to myself.

'She said she can get free drinks, too. But I'm not sure that's a *proper* superpower,' Lucy says, with a comically serious expression on her face.

I guide her ahead of me on a narrow stretch, happy I can laugh without her seeing my face. Elaine is a female cad, whatever that is called. I'm sure she last paid for a drink in 1989.

We emerge onto the straight from the hairpin bend, and the racetrack slows down. At the top of the hill, the pavement widens like a smile. The entrance to the Modern Art Gallery comes into sight, and I wish this was our destination today. The driveway tunnels through an archway of trees. Green grass terraces like rice paddies curve above a glassy moat in front of the Georgian building. This manmade sculpture is Lucy's second favourite thing about the museum. Her favourite is the café where she drinks hot chocolate and lets her feet swing back and forth beneath the chair.

She breaks away from me again, her skinny legs pistoning beneath her school kilt when the iron man comes into view. This cast-iron sculpture by Anthony Gormley, brown with age, is buried up to the chest in tarmac. Well, that's what Lucy believes.

'No one would make half a man. That's silly, daddy. How would you know where to stop? One day I'll be big enough to pull him out. Then you'll see.'

I hope I am there to witness this when she does, King Arthur style.

Today, she takes a run-up, places her hands on the cold, bald head, and leapfrogs over the top. Her bunches bounce when she lands, and she's laughing so hard that her nose starts to run. She looks over at me to check. No need to worry. Her joy is infectious; I am laughing, too. For good measure, because she must detect my mood, she makes another circuit, leaping over the man again. Her giggles drown out the din of traffic, my worries, my fears.

'Bravo!' I clap and laugh. My shoulders drop and my face hurts from smiling so much; I could cry with gratitude and relief.

I check my watch, but Lucy trots back to my side like the good kid she is. Hand in hand, we cross the road. The school gates are in sight.

'So, Lucy Goosey,' I ask before we say our goodbyes. 'You haven't told me what *your* superpower is.'

She grins wide enough that I can see the gap where a molar is missing. 'Daddy.' Shyly, she pulls on the front of my coat. 'You *know* my superpower.'

The clock is ticking. I have to get to work, but for the life of me, I cannot hurry this child. 'Maybe you can whisper it to me,' I say, mesmerised by the shine in her eyes and the bashful pink of her cheeks.

She nods her head vigorously, and I bend down until we are level. 'My superpower is making you laugh,' she whispers, bumping her nose into my cheek before she pushes me away when we hear the thunder of children's feet and someone calling her name.

I watch, speechless, as Lucy waves without looking back. She links arms with Ethan and a tiny new girl whose name I think is Rhona. 'Bye, Dad,' she yells before they run away towards the entrance. 'Have a good day.'

'Bye, Lucy Goosey,' I whisper, because by then she is gone.

The doors to the hospice shush open and I walk inside with a lightness that feels new. Too soon, the odour of cooked food and overheated air smothers me. I cling to the joy my daughter brought to our morning commute.

'Morning, Maggie.' I wave at the volunteer manning the hospice shop before taking the stairs two at a time.

'Mister Cunningham isn't doing so well,' a fellow nurse says as we fall in step along the white-washed corridor.

'Bad night? Has the doctor been around?'

'He hasn't eaten since yesterday. His daughter tried to give him cereal earlier, but he couldn't keep it down.' She checks her chunky watch. 'He had another seizure about an hour ago. Doctor's due any minute.'

Mr. Cunningham has a brain tumour, a glioblastoma multiforme, the worst kind. He's been here for two weeks. Golf course to a neurology ward and on to us in the space of nine days.

'What are we talking? Days? Hours?' I ask.

'You're better at that than I am,' Peggy says. 'Pop your head in when you get a chance.'

I drop my things in the locker room and find Mr. Cunningham's daughter sitting in the armchair beside his bed. She's holding her father's bone-pale hand, her thumb caressing a shiny bulb of knuckle. His eyes are closed, chest barely moving beneath the colourful crocheted blanket one of the hospice volunteers has made.

'Morning, Heather,' I say. 'I hear Dad had a difficult night. How're you doing today?'

Heather is somewhere in her thirties, an elegant woman who takes care of her appearance come what may. More than once, I've walked in as she touched up her lipstick.

Not vain, merely clinging to a little normality in a world that has suddenly spun out of control.

She looks at her father's face and gently shakes her head. 'He seemed so good yesterday after you moved him to this lovely private room. He watched the news while I fed him lunch. We talked about the earthquakes in Turkey and Syria. He looked at my phone when I showed him pictures of the kids. He smiled at me. I thought maybe…we were turning a…'

She trails off and, in that moment, I know what she's thinking. Maybe the doctors got it wrong, maybe her dad will defy the odds. By some miracle, he will recover from this, the worst kind of diagnosis. But she's a smart woman; she cannot lie to herself. Not even for a moment.

'Yesterday.' I tilt my head and purse my lips, careful about what I am about to say.

'The rallying you saw, his energy and engagement…'

'Yes,' she nods, smiling again, hungry for anything other than the news I am about to deliver.

'It's called terminal lucidity, Heather.'

'Terminal lucidity?' she repeats, sagging as the meaning dawns and the air leaves her lungs like deflated balloons.

'It's a stage some terminal patients go through. A surge of energy, clarity.'

'Before…' She chews her lip and bows her head, resigned this time.

Her focus swings back to her dad, his eyes closed as he sleeps. I leave the room; she doesn't need me now. She doesn't hear me go.

I make my rounds, refilling water jugs, wiping dribbles from unshaven chins, and worse. I feel Lucy's lightness fading, so I force myself to revisit our morning walk, to picture my daughter's smile, to plumb my memory for her laughter.

A couple of hours later, I watch Heather walk towards the stairs. She is upright but her steps are slower than usual. She's going home to Glasgow. She's been making the ninety-mile round trip every day for the past week. Her devotion touches me; not every hospice patient is so lucky.

Afternoon shifts towards evening. The fading light sets off a dementia patient, this sundowning effect making him agitated. I put soothing music on the radio in the four-bed ward. I light lamps with warm-toned bulbs that throw blush tones around the room. A cup of tea and a quiet chat and gradually the man begins to settle. Shadows no longer look like monsters he must fight off.

I pause outside Mr. Cunningham's room. We moved him to this single-bed suite yesterday to give the patient and the family privacy. Heather thanked us for being so generous, but I think, deep down, she knows.

When I check on him, his body is convulsing, again. A brown-red liquid leaks from his nose as he seizes, a sign that the tumour is breaking down. I stay with him until the seizure stops and then I clean him up. With help, I change the sheets and make him comfortable.

'I'm going to call his daughter,' I tell my colleague, Jo.

Heather answers on the second ring. She sounds a little breathless.

'How soon can you come in?' I know she'll wade through hell and high water to make it to her father's bedside. 'It's almost time. You should come if you can.'

Heather must break the speed limit and run every light. Not an hour later, she runs down the hushed corridor with her husband trailing in her wake.

Robert Cunningham sighs his last not two hours after that. Heather is by his side. She holds his hand and whispers her love as the air rattles out of his chest and the room becomes newly still.

I check his vitals one last time. Heather hugs me in the hallway, thanking me for everything with tears shining in her eyes.

I open my locker at the end of shift. As I shrug on my coat, I wonder if *this* is my superpower – this ability to foresee the end, to deliver loved ones to one another for a final farewell. I am not unhappy if that is the case, though I think I will spare Lucy Goosey this news for now. At least until she is a little older.

Cold snap later, with falling iguanas
by Hazel Osmond

Longlisted, Edinburgh Award for Flash Fiction 2023

After breakfast Gran would tap on Barry's glass, look at his pointy hands, and say, 'Right, beach it is,' or, 'Board games inside,' or even, 'Now, where did I put that sledge?'

But one morning she said, 'Cold snap later, with falling iguanas.'

They came down just after lunch – great green and red ones, the frills under their chins all wobbly. We caught them in the laundry basket and put them in the airing cupboard, wrapped in foil.

Next day, it was 'High temperatures in Antarctica, overheating penguins by noon.'

Gran sailed the sofa over the lawn while I hauled Emperors and Gentoo on board in a blanket. When Mum arrived back from work, they were torpedoing figures-of-eight through the ice cubes in the bath.

By Friday, there were turtle eggs in the sandpit and lemurs in the greenhouse. Armadillos scratched around the loft.

'Just need to make a quick phone call,' Mum said, patting my shoulder, and a man came and shone a light in Gran's eyes. Whatever he saw in her head, it meant she had to go straight to bed and stay there.

But, that night, I heard *tap-tap-tap* from downstairs.

We found Gran lying out by the compost bins, her hands as blue as her dressing gown.

'Floods imminent,' she whispered. 'Lift the worms.'

Now Gran has gone away, I need Barry to tell me what animals I should save next, but he's turned his little face to the wall.

Sea Change
by Livia Dyring

Longlisted, Edinburgh Award for Flash Fiction 2023

Her father was dead.

She had pushed the creaking door open and seen how light had illuminated not him but a corpse, the first she had ever seen. The sun had risen, but he had not, and never would again. Though the physical matter that made the body – skin, bones, blood – remained, the vessel was suddenly dry as the desert.

Word spread, and men knocked on the door. They would come again tomorrow, they said.

That day was the longest she had ever lived. She sat by him until nightfall. He seemed peaceful, but she saw the toil, how the salty seas had stretched his leathery skin tautly over his cheekbones. She felt an urge to reach out and lift his eyelids, so that she could see the color of his irises one more time. Those eyes had always been blue and light even when the water was hard and dark.

When faint light began shimmering above the water, she knew that the time had come. Soon they would be here with saws and hammers. Tradition was as eternal as the waves they sailed upon, and when an old fisherman died, their house was demolished and the wooden boards transformed into a new boat. Then the body was put inside, and the tide would take the vessel and its lone sailor out – returned to the thundering cold waters where everything had begun.

She squeezed the inanimate hand only once. Then she walked out the door.

Dancing Away
by Caroline Vevers

Longlisted, Edinburgh Award for Flash Fiction 2023

Grace floated down the ballroom's staircase, taking centre position in an entourage of adoring men. She knew she looked stunning in a dazzling white, deceptively simple, designer cocktail dress. A silver link chain ran from one shoulder across to her narrow waist. Long, shapely legs and toned slim arms completed her film star look. Her fiancé, my dad-to-be, Jerry, looked on from the side in awe at the prize within his grasp. It's black and white, of course. Above their heads the banner reads, 'Happy New Year – 1963'.

'I loved dancing with your dad,' she smiled as she looked longingly at the photo. She shifted uneasily. Her back was hurting again. She'd hardly slept. The doctor had told her, even with the recent operation and pacemaker, her heart was failing. Her once beautiful legs were now swollen with fluid her body could no longer flush out. The skin was broken, spotty and irritated. Fluid seeped through the skin on her legs. The dressings to soak it up just exaggerated the swelling.

I looked at the congealing food in front of her. Soggy pie, gravy wrinkling around saggy broccoli and greying mash. Her cup of tea had developed a skin. Milk swirled with age underneath the surface. Grace attempted to get up with her stick.

'Ach, stay there Mum. I'll take it through for you.'

When I came back through she'd gone. Someone else was slumped in the seat. But the photo was in her outstretched hand. Grace had gone dancing.

The Well
by Jake Zarak

Longlisted, Edinburgh Award for Flash Fiction 2023

I blink grime out of my eyes. A thin ray of moonlight slips over me, illuminating damp dirt dotted with tiny puddles. Around me, frogs and insects move through darkness with soft squelching. I rest against a rough cobble wall that stretches all the way up to the lip of the well. Stars can be seen through that small circle, salt dusted over darkness. I pull my patched blue coat tight, these nights are cold. My father lowers me down here everytime the sun dips below the horizon, and raises me out everytime day breaks. It's not always the well; some nights we sneak onto a boat, he lowers it until I can reach the river. He doesn't like it when I play with the water, the splashes echo too loud in the night's silence. In the well I can't see flashes from the town, nor the blinking lights in the sky, I can only hear the explosions, the screams of the fighter jets. I swallow and try to wrap myself even tighter in my coat, ignoring the constant wail of the siren. Dirt thrown up from the bombs sprinkles into the well and dusts my hair. I shut my eyes and pray for the morning, for my father's smile above, please, please come back.

Fractals
by Jennie Higgs

Longlisted, Edinburgh Short Story Award 2023

His hand moved quickly but precisely. Eyes firmly fixed on the task. Attention unwavering. I was poised. Trying to anticipate what he would need next. My eyes also focused but flicking back and forth between the tray, ready to hand him the next implement. I thought I could see a problem coming and found myself caught in uncertainty. My hesitation made him pause too as he calculated options. I tried to pass him what I thought he needed but a firm shake of the head and a flick of his hand in the direction of the tray corrected me. I placed it firmly in his palm. He registered nothing, his focus absolute. I had completely disconnected from everything else now, could not have said in that moment what else was happening around us. All my attention was on him, his hands, his steady focused gaze. A crease formed between his straight dark eyebrows, and I leaned closer, trying to see what had provoked his concern. There, just at the edge, something not quite right. Not a catastrophe, not yet, but enough to pull his concentration towards it. I did not suppose this time to know what he needed but waited with hand hovering over the tray until a new flick of his hand advised me. I expected no thanks, no acknowledgement, not now in this crucial moment. Then, it was done. He leant back, eyes taking in the whole scene, the crease of worry easing. He did not smile but a calm settled over his face and his eyes flicked up to mine then away, then back again before resting on the image in front of him.

'Beautiful,' his mother said, and she rapped her knuckle twice on the table, 'well done.' The boy reached out and 'rat-tap' knocked twice too. A signal, a communication. His mother smiled, her face momentarily brightening before falling back into tired lines. She shifted the sleeping baby in her arms and raised her eyes to mine. 'Thank you, that was very kind,' she murmured.

The boy's drawing lay between us. The image caught me, drew me in. The patterns and shapes, the repeating and fragmenting lines. It was like a fern, or a film of ice creeping along a window, or possibly a tree. The lines rendered so precisely that it seemed impossible that his frantic hand had kept them so neat. There was a name for these patterns, but I could not get my brain to dredge it up. The colours too were incredible, the warm reds of the top left corner shifting and blending to end in cool blues at the bottom right. The urgency that had been so evident in the making had gone and a calm orderliness replaced it. I felt an odd mix of exhilaration and embarrassment at my absorption. The woman and I sat and continued to stare at the image, but the boy had shifted his attention to the landscape rushing past outside the window. His finger tapped on the table in some private rhythm. Keeping time.

When I had first boarded the train, the heat had hit me instantly. The platform, though in full afternoon sun, had been blessed by a breeze that was absent on the train. I felt sweat prickle at my hairline and the skin on my arms and back started to itch where it was in contact with my jumper. As I had paused to allow an elderly man to get his bearings, I had held my hand over a vent. The air wheezing out of it was warm. The smell hit me next, reminding me why I hated joining trains part way through the journey. You didn't notice the heady mix of toilet chemicals, warm bodies, egg mayonnaise and stale coffee if it crept up around you from the start. It was stepping into it ready-made that made my nose wrinkle. I had been tutted at then, by a woman in a suit who I bet would be regretting her outfit choice before the train had cleared the station, and realised I was hovering in the vestibule. I tried to orientate myself to the seat layout and my stomach lurched. I was certain that I had picked a forward-facing seat in a pair, but my ticket was unmistakably directing me to a backward seat at a table. The two seats opposite were already occupied. The woman's cheeks were flushed, and a strand of blonde hair clung to her forehead. Her eyes were glassy as she stared into the middle distance. She held a baby, green sleep suit adorned with a pattern of dinosaurs, long lashes sweeping her cheeks in deep sleep. The boy was by the window. He looked about ten, angular, elbows improbably sharp looking and visible below the short sleeves of his bright red t-shirt. His thin face was pale and surrounded by bright blonde hair that swept his shoulders, but his eyes were dark.

I settled into the seat and tried to focus on the relief of going home, another trip to see my mother and stepfather endured and incident free aside from a row about my hair. Pink was evidently not my colour. A high-pitched squeal dragged me back to my surroundings. The teenagers across the aisle were trading gossip but whether the squeal was delight or disgust I didn't know. Behind them two small boys played a video game on a handheld device with no headphones, volume loud, the parent ignoring disapproving looks by resolutely staring at his phone. The fabric of the seat was rough but the itching from my jumper had intensified and so I struggled out of it. I pulled the bobble out of my hair and redid my ponytail higher, trying to keep my damp hair from my neck. Headphones on, I pressed play and tried to let the 'chill out' playlist work its magic. Outside the window we were still in the outskirts of the city, but nature was trying its best to mask the derelict buildings and disused railway machinery with long grass and tangled shrubs. My eye caught on some graffiti improbably high up on a partially ruined warehouse. The train picked up speed.

The boy was staring out the window too, his eyes travelling and then flicking back, drifting then flicking back. His left hand was on the table and his index finger lifted and tapped, lifted and tapped in some rhythm which seemed to be related to outside. I watched and realised he was counting out electricity poles. I studied his face for a few moments and saw a twitching around his jaw line. Tension or an involuntary tic, I couldn't tell. The rest of him was still. Just his eyes, his index finger and the left side of his jaw moved. He was extraordinarily focused.

The tannoy crackled and spat into life startling the boy from his reverie. I shifted headphones away from one ear and listened. The announcement concerned catering; a list seemingly comprised of sandwich fillings that they did not have in stock delivered so rapidly as to be almost unintelligible. Apparently in response the baby started to wail. Tiny fists screwed up, arms rigid in the irrational anger peculiar to babies. The boy froze, eyes no longer scanning. His mother, while trying to soothe the baby, said to the boy, voice tight with forced brightness, 'Would you like a snack love?' The boy said nothing and, as the baby's wails intensified, covered his ears and began to rock back and forth. My stomach dropped and I felt my face grow hot. I determinedly fixed my eyes outside the window but knew other people were looking. My scalp prickled.

The mother leaned down into her bag and quickly pulled out a pad of drawing paper and a metal box of coloured pencils. She placed the paper in front of her son and said, voice still trying for cheery brightness, 'Come on lovie, why don't you do me a picture while I sort out Isla.' One-handed she prised the lid of the pencils and tried to rummage for one of them. Her hand slipped and the red pencil fell and landed under the table. The boy was making a noise now, a low humming that was in time with the rocking. The teenagers at the table across the aisle appeared to be in pain from trying not to laugh.

Instinctively I pulled off my headphones, leant down and plucked the pencil from the grubby carpet. I sat up and proffered it to the boy. For a moment nothing happened and then he reached out and snatched it from me and started to draw. The lines were frantic at first and I wondered if he would rip the paper but then he steadied, finding a flow. I shot an uncertain glance at his mother, but she smiled gratefully, mouthed 'thank you' and continued feeding the baby. The boy and I settled into a rhythm of passing pencils between us and my role as his assistant continued until he wordlessly declared it complete.

As he went back to staring out of the window, I watched his face again. The twitching in his jaw had stopped and his face was serene as his eyes scanned the countryside that was now passing outside. I glanced across at the woman again, a tightness in my chest, my eyes hot. She was stroking the baby's head, apparently totally absorbed but I could tell she was fully aware of the boy. I joined him in his observation of the trees.

'I really appreciated you doing that,' she said calmly, startlingly me out of my reverie. 'James loves to draw.' The many unsaid things hovered for a moment and then she looked away, reaching for her phone. Wordlessly I put my headphones back on and lifted my own phone. Fractals. That was what the patterns were. The online definition was heavy with ratios and equations. I struggled to make sense of it so clicked away to the images. Beautiful examples from nature mingled with impossibly intricate designs rendered on computers. The animations were mesmerising, the lines dividing and connecting, endlessly spooling onwards. I drifted.

Movement snagged my attention. The mother was gathering belongings while trying not to jostle the baby. The tinny voice from the tannoy announced the next stop. Indecision gripped my chest, should I say something, should I just smile and nod. My lower back felt slick with sweat, the skin on my arms itched again against the seat and my headphones felt tight. I pulled them off and said, my voice feeling constricted in my throat, 'Nice to have met you,' my face flushed. The mother was trying to cram the last few items into her bag but glanced up, her eyes soft, 'You too.' To her son she said, 'Come on James love, grandad will be waiting. Bring your picture.' He said nothing, and they started to move towards the door.

The platform was busy, people unhelpfully crowding around the doors rather than letting people have space to disembark, everyone seemed to have a large suitcase. The train was going to get even fuller. I focused instead on the hanging baskets running the entire length of the platform. The rainbow hued petunias and tumbling fuchsias were resplendent, the symmetry of the petals now revealed to me. Nature endlessly repeating.

'Rat-tap' two knocks on the table beside me. I glanced across. James' picture lay in front of me, his blonde head and bright red t-shirt already retreating down the aisle and off towards the door.

The Last Dance
by Gill Sherry

Longlisted, Edinburgh Award for Flash Fiction 2023

This was not how he'd envisaged celebrating fifty years of marriage. Yet, here they were, clinging to each other in a makeshift bomb shelter, frightened for their lives as explosions rocked their beloved city.

The cracked face of his pocket watch, a wedding gift from Yulia, confirmed it was nine pm. He pictured the church hall full of balloons and flowers; friends and family in their new frocks, best suits and polished shoes; the handsome cake with a golden '50' atop; half a century of smiles beaming down from the montage of photographs on the wall.

His foot tapped under their shared blanket as he imagined dancing to the three-piece band, guiding Yulia around the floor, her blue eyes shining.

Nothing shone in the metro station, the faintest rays of hope doused by dust and debris. Dogs whimpered, children cried, one man openly prayed.

He took a sip of water from a plastic bottle. There would be no champagne tonight, no glasses held aloft. Just the bitter taste of dread and despair.

A hush descended in the tunnel. He became aware of the faint sound of music, the atmosphere in the cold shelter warming to the strings of a violin, expertly played by a stranger.

He took Yulia's trembling hand, coaxed her to her feet, encouraged her with a smile. A familiar twinkle appeared in her eyes as she nodded her understanding. A ripple of applause followed and, for the very last time, they danced.

Dealbreaker
by Ann Seed

Longlisted, Edinburgh Award for Flash Fiction 2023

'Barney-2,' Alfie sobbed, 'He's dead. Just like Barney-1.'
'Sorry, son,' said Brian.
'But I really want a puppy, dad.'
'I know. But remember… a deal's a deal.'
'I can do it, dad. I can.'
'Please don't cry, son. You can try again. I promise.'

Brian kissed Alfie goodnight then trudged downstairs. He grabbed his Prozac pills and gulped one down with a whisky. Afterwards, he tipped the fish-tank water into the toilet along with Barney-2. 'Sorry, mate,' he whispered.

Next morning, as usual, he walked through the saleroom, transfixed by the gleaming new vehicles. Outside, the mob of used cars jostled for his attention. They looked as frayed as his cuffs… as dismal as his sales figures… as grim as his promotion prospects… as battered as his overdraft…

Weeks later, after much pleading, Brian agreed to let Alfie choose a new goldfish. The tank spotless, filter purring, a beaming Alfie placed his charge in the dechlorinated water and carefully measured *'the optimal amount of food to maintain good health.'*

'Don't worry, Barney-3, I'll look after you. I'll prove I'm responsible. Then I'll get my puppy.'

Alfie safely in bed, Brian reinstated the nightly ritual. He emptied the fish-tank, filled it with tap water and threw in more food. Barney-3 ate greedily.

Brian clutched his Prozac. They made him shine like a new car. For a moment. Before the tears. Poor Alfie… he was barking at the Moon. Barney-10 or 100… it didn't matter… no sales, no puppy… no anything…

Concrete Evidence
by Celia Donovan

Longlisted, Edinburgh Award for Flash Fiction 2023

It's nae easy, you ken, being a cement block at the bottom of the Clyde; my body of limestone and clay, wrapped in chains, wedged in sludge and strapped tae a plastic sarcophagus. I dinnae ken the previous owner of the bones encased within, but they are sentient no more. We are shackled here thegither but say nocht most days.

Occasionally an involuntary belch escapes between the layers of decomposing matter in his carrier bag helmet, but like a decrepit auld timer in a care home, he disnae ken which way is up. The tide works its way around u, although we dance to its schedule.

My brethren haul up the foundations of schools fae Orkney tae Arran, watch ageing ankles in support bandages pass by all day at the bowling greens, or laze, spray painted yellae, propping up rusty cars in the scrap yard.

But trapped underwater is my destiny, wi the rest of the non-perishables. It's a murky soup; there's the heavyweights like masel who gan naewhere fast; shopping trolleys and tyres mostly. Beer cans and used jonnies and crisp packets commute frae a to b, then the fresh meat that's already passed its best, lopsided trout and dead gulls and occasional wan eyed eels shuffling by. The tourists we call them. You've got tae keep your sense of humour in this game, and there's nae room for envy in this business, nane at aw. You've got tae have thick skin; concrete is thicker than water, after all.

The Apology
by Emma Henderson

Longlisted, Edinburgh Short Story Award 2023

Phoebe O'Shaughnessy wore a bra. I didn't. We didn't. We were eleven, going on twelve. Phoebe O'Shaughnessy showed us her bra, during break, on our first day at secondary school – an all-girls' grammar in Hammersmith, with a catchment area stretching from Paddington and the rich borough of Kensington, right out to the south and west London sticks of Wimbledon, Richmond, Ealing and Hounslow. In from the sticks came suburban, semi-detached people like me, and clever, council-estate kids like my friend, Beryl. We were the District and Piccadilly line girls. We were the 27, 91 and 267 bus afficionados.

Phoebe O'Shaughnessy wasn't one of these. She travelled out to Hammersmith with the posh girls from Kensington, Chelsea, Notting Hill Gate. They'd attended private prep schools, already possessed a smattering of Latin and French, and had holidayed 'on the continent', as my parents would say, not Cornwall (me) or Butlins (Beryl).

We crowded round Phoebe O'Shaughnessy in the cloakroom on that first day, as she removed her tie and undid the top three buttons of her school blouse. The bra was pale, blue-and-white checked cotton. Sort of gingham. Sort of thrilling.

'You can get them in yellow and white,' said Phoebe O'Shaughnessy, rebuttoning her blouse. 'And pink and white. From John Lewis. My stepmother bought me one of each.'

'Stepmother?' I couldn't help querying. Until that memorable day in early September 1969, I'd only knowingly come across stepmothers in fairy tales. As to bras, those were the large, heavy beige contraptions belonging to Mum, pegged weekly on the washing line.

'Stacey's my second stepmother.' Phoebe O'Shaughnessy elaborated. 'She's an actress.

From California. She's twenty-five. My real mamma died yonks ago. Papa's a philanderer. That's what Nanny says.'

I had no idea and didn't ask what a philanderer was. My dad was a banker, and Beryl's worked at the Walls ice-cream factory in Acton. Our mums were housewives.

For the next five years, Phoebe O'Shaugnessy and I were in the same tutor group, and the same sets for maths and French, so our paths crossed, our shoulders rubbed, our circles sometimes overlapped. We weren't friends. We weren't enemies. The posh girls more or less claimed Phoebe O'Shaughnessy as one of their own. And she was willing, when she wanted, to be the leader of this clique. But she often remained apart; not aloof exactly, just alone. The rest of us fell into vague and various friendship groups, based arbitrarily on seating plans, travel arrangements, chance and desperation.

My fate didn't really intertwine with Phoebe O'Shaughnessy's until our O-level year. Nevertheless, I remember a lot about Phoebe O'Shaughnessy prior to that. Here are just some of the things I remember.

She was bright. Lazy, cheeky, charming, bright. A's in English and maths. A+'s in art.

She was funny. On April 1st, that first year, every single board rubber in the school disappeared. They were those chunky wooden blocks, about six inches long, with hard grey felt on the underside. We – and the teachers – occasionally threw them. There were two in every classroom and boxes of spares in the stationery cupboard. Phoebe O'Shaughnessy nicked them all. I don't know when or how she did it, but she laid them on the playing field, which was overlooked by the staffroom and the dining hall. And with the board rubbers, she spelt out, in large letters, the words, 'April Fool'. Even the teachers had the grace to laugh, I remember.

She was deliciously pretty, with long-lashed, brown berry-eyes, cherry-red lips, freckles and dark chestnut curls. She had an impish grin, which was a tiny bit toothy. Her body wasn't perfect. It was round and stumpy, untannably pale, and she was slightly pigeon-toed. But she carried herself confidently, energetically and could do a great imitation of the Pan's People dancers on Top of the Pops.

She was helpful. By the end of the third year, most of us had started our period. We struggled with bulky belts and pads or, if we were lucky, Kotex stick-ons. Until Phoebe O'Shaughnessy, knickerless and one foot up on the toilet seat, introduced us to the virtues of the tampon.

She was a diet and beauty expert. She swore that toothpaste worked better than Clearasil on spots, and she wore thick woolly tights on the hottest days of the year. She said it was a sure-fire way of losing weight.

She was generous. In June 1973, when we were fourteen going on fifteen, she invited the whole class to the musical *Hair* at the Shaftesbury theatre in the West End. Beryl's parents didn't let her go, because of the nudity. The nudity was disappointing: just hairy men and skinny women wandering around the stage, holding hands and singing.

And last but not least, Phoebe O'Shaughnessy was, as she herself put it, 'full of Irish surprises'. For example, she said she earned a massive fifty quid a week over the summer, that summer after *Hair*, washing dead bodies in a mortuary owned by an aunt in Galway.

By the beginning of our O-level year, Phoebe O'Shaughnessy had a Saturday job on a stall in Kensington Market – all patchouli oil, joss sticks, cheesecloth and tie-dye. In her lunch hour, she regularly shoplifted clothes from Biba. I had a Saturday job in the M&S on Ealing High Street and once, in my lunch hour, shoplifted a copy of Wilfred Owen's poems from WHSmith. I hung out with boys from the boys' grammar school, who quoted Nietzsche, smoked dope and listened to Bob Dylan. By Christmas, I was officially going out with one of them and I was on the pill, skipping school to canoodle and all the rest of it.

Phoebe O'Shaughnessy was on the pill and skipping school too. She was in with a crowd of art-school students, men not boys, who did speed and LSD and paid her a pound to model for their life-drawing class. But Phoebe O'Shaughnessy went further than that:

'I'm shagging their tutor,' she said. 'Jasper Pennington. He's a friend of Papa's. I've known him all my life. He's quite a famous painter, you know.'

We were rumbled in March. Miss Bradshaw, who taught us maths, eventually noticed a pattern of absenteeism and had the nouse to phone our homes, only to discover we weren't there, we weren't sick. Oh no! We were in big trouble.

'Your teachers are insulted,' the headmistress said.

'Insulted?' I puzzled. There had been no intention to upset, let alone insult, no thought whatsoever, in fact, of anyone else's feelings.

'Yes. Insulted. They all refuse to teach you.'

'So you're expelling us?' said Phoebe O'Shaughnessy.

'Well, no. I wouldn't say that.'

'But you are.'

'Not exactly.'

'You are.'

'No.'

'Yes.'

It was a stand-off. Individually, the teachers refused to teach us. And yet the school refused to expel us. For a couple of weeks, in the run-up to Easter, Phoebe O'Shaughnessy and I became a kind of *cause célèbre*. We behaved as if we were somehow the wounded party. We turned up at school, correctly attired, on time, every day. Instead of attending lessons, we sat in a warm sunny nook in the library. We sat there very publicly, very together. We shared – sandwiches, magazines, snippets of our lives and, above all, our silly, righteous, adolescent indignation.

After more than a week of this, and as the novelty of the situation wore off, Miss Bradshaw came to talk to us.

'Look,' she said. 'All you have to do is apologise. Apologise to each teacher, one by one. And they'll let you back in. That's it. That's all. I guarantee.'

She was persuasive. We said we'd think about it.

We talked about it.

I did it.

I'm sorry. I'm sorry. I'm sorry.

Phoebe O'Shaughnessy didn't.

I'm sorry.

We broke up for the Easter holidays and Phoebe O'Shaughnessy never returned to school. I sat my O-levels, stayed on for A-levels and went off to university.

Ten months later, I was temping for the summer as a secretary in central London. I often bought a copy of the Evening Standard to read on the tube home. It made me feel like a proper Londoner, not the scaredy-cat, cowardly arriviste I knew I really was. Piccadilly Circus, Green Park, Hyde Park Corner, Knightsbridge. It was between Knightsbridge and South Kensington station that I read about Phoebe O'Shaughnessy's death. By the time I got off the train at Hounslow West, I'd read the short article over and over. There was her name. There was her photo. It was a horrible death. She'd been crushed by a lorry in Soho. A garbage truck, to be precise. It had happened in the small hours. Pronounced dead upon arrival at Barts. The details were sickening. She'd been high. She'd been crawling along Dean Street, giggling, according to a passer-by. She'd lain down behind the truck for a joke, according to a friend. It had reversed over her. The article said Phoebe O'Shaughnessy was enrolled at St Martin's School of Art, but hadn't been seen there for weeks. She was a regular user, according to the friend. An addict. Blah, blah.

I blamed myself. Of course I did. A bit. What if? What if she hadn't left school? What if she'd done the apology thing? I'd always felt as if I'd somehow sold out, abased myself by going to the teachers with my dishonest sorries. I remember entering the library afterwards, flushed with success and the effort of insincerity, seeing Phoebe, her head bent in concentration over *Jackie* magazine, her dark curls backlit by the sun.

'Piece of piss,' I swaggered over to her. 'You should do it.'

'No,' said Phoebe O'Shaughnessy. 'Not on your life.'

She didn't. I did.

She died. I didn't.

And that should have been the story of Phoebe O'Shaughnessy. Except there's a little epilogue.

Job, husband, kids, empty nest, divorce. In 2014, I found myself, in my mid-fifties, having a fling with a wealthy widower in New York. One afternoon, while he was at work, I dawdled aimlessly around Chinatown and the Lower East Side. The place teemed with trendy new art galleries, and my attention was caught by a poster for a retrospective of the British painter, Jasper Pennington. The name gave me a jolt as I remembered its connection with Phoebe O'Shaugnessy, and, despite certain misgivings, I felt compelled to enter the gallery. The catalogue confirmed that Jasper Pennington had taught at St Martin's in the seventies and early eighties. There were nudes galore from that period – great, glorious, oily bodies, male and female, garish colours, all shapes and sizes – but not a sign of Phoebe O'Shaughnessy in any of them. Relieved and disappointed in equal measure, I made my way to Pennington's later paintings, which were even bigger and more abstract and meant nothing to me. But near the exit was a small side room containing his early work, and here was a more pleasing, more accessible collection of landscapes, portraits and still-lifes. And here was a painting of Phoebe O'Shaughnessy. Not the drug-addled, garbage-truck Phoebe O'Shaughnessy. Not even the teenage, speed-taking Phoebe O'Shaughnessy. This was a young girl, scarcely pubescent, sitting on a bench on a lawn, against a backdrop of roses and honeysuckle. The setting was enchanting, the lines delicate, the colours pastel. The girl wore a pale, blue-and-white, checked cotton bra and nothing else at all. Zero, nix, zilch. Her legs were splayed. Her hands were hidden beneath an open book on her lap. The implication of what Phoebe O'Shaughnessy might be doing with her hands would have shocked me, had I not been so struck by her face, which betrayed nothing untoward. There was no ecstasy or disgust, just the shiniest of looks in her eye and that tiny-bit-toothy, impish smile. Pennington had perfectly captured the bright, berry-cherry, chestnutty, cheeky eleven-year-old Phoebe O'Shaughnessy, in all her innocence and tragic, precocious experience. The title of painting, dated circa 1969, was 'The Apology'.

Census, 1841
by Kristina Sutherland

Longlisted, Edinburgh Award for Flash Fiction 2023

I want you to be remembered, recorded and recognised.

I rushed to answer when the schoolmaster knocked on our door at supper time. The house was alive with routines but we both left the bairns to it for this occasion.

'William Cow, forty…a fisherman…at's richt enough, another een.'

He looked over at me. 'Wife, Margaret, forty… Liskie, she's fifteen, Weelam's twelve, Andra's ten, Wee Muggie's acht, Rab's sax, Mary's fower, Ann's twa, i baby's Bella and she's acht month last wik.' I was proud as he reeled off our bairns, and all their ages. As if I'd not been reciting the list for him, rehearsing for this moment.

You peeled away from me, all blood and sinew, thirteen years ago. My body has not forgotten you. The sense of your weight leaving the place where you should have thrived as you splashed into the pot below me. The pain began between my legs, but it festered and took root in the part of me that is for mothering. At first you lived in the shame that I could not keep you and the worry that you would be the last. Then you lingered in the late night 'what ifs', like this one.

My grandaughter's great-grandaughter will see the names of your brothers and sisters piled up after your father's and then mine. Will she notice that the siblings are all born twenty four months apart except for Liskie who's three years older than the rest?

Your absence is your legacy.

Tree
by Thomas Caldow

Longlisted, Edinburgh Short Story Award 2023

When my girlfriend first told me she planned on becoming a tree I am ashamed to admit that I did not take her entirely seriously. It was a night much like this one, or any other for that matter, and we had passed the day in much the same way as all the others before it, so it seemed slightly absurd to be told amidst all that mundanity that my partner was planning a new path of existence.

As a person there was not much particularly arboreal about her. She had definitely been described as flinty, yes, and at times even icy, but you would have been hard pressed to find anyone who described her as leafy. My first thought, as you can imagine with all the facts at your disposal, was that life as a tree did not seem like it would suit her.

'But you're a person'

'I understand that, but I've had enough, I feel like becoming a tree'

'But where will you stay? What will you do for work? I'm not sure a tree is welcome behind a bar.'

'I'll live wherever I find some earth where I can put down my roots, and as far as I can tell from my research, trees don't have jobs and don't seem too interested in finding them either.'

This was when I first began to suspect that I should be taking this more seriously than I had thought. While we were largely happy to move in circles we knew and understood, when she did pick up a new interest or obsession, my girlfriend would spend many nights hunched behind her laptop exploring the subject till she knew all there was to know about it. The only time we had been on holiday together over the course of our relationship, we walked down the wide streets of Paris side by side as she explained the history of every brick, window and local off-licence. When I think about it now, all I remember were the boulevards lined with trees.

She had become excited by Paris, so it seemed only natural that she would become a scholar of the city, and that she would then go and see it. For the ten days we were there she was in every sense of the word a Parisian. She had a system and she followed it. All of a sudden it did not seem that far-fetched to me that if she applied the same level of dedication to her latest pursuit she could well be a tree before the year was through. This realisation did not sit comfortably with me. Far more than simply an issue of taste (I had always found her to be a beautiful woman, I was not confident I would feel the same about a tree), there was another question that had appeared in my mind but that I was unable to voice: 'What about me?'

I had had the exact same thought seven years previously, on the night I first met her. Between underage draws of shoplifted cigarettes, she had told me she was going home. It wasn't till a week later when I got her text that I had my answer. And so it went, a daring statement, followed by my pause, till eventually, a moment, day, week, month later, she answered for me. Throughout that entire time I'm not sure I ever took a step, I was always carried.

So that evening, with the question burning in the air between us, I instead asked, 'What tree will you be?'

As far as she was concerned there was only one right answer: the poplar. 'But', she said, 'I am going to lay out to you exactly how I got to that decision.

'At first I had considered an evergreen, like a Scots Pine maybe. They are some of the biggest in the world and keep their needles all year round so I'd never get cold even standing head and shoulders (she was still thinking like a human) above all my friends in the forest.

'But I have never really liked the feel of the needles. And more importantly, if I had my needles all year round I'd never

174

get to feel what it's like to bud and to blossom. So I thought I might become a cherry tree. Do you remember the way my street in Glasgow would look come March? A whole street of whites and pinks! But as soon as I thought about it I remembered how quickly the blossom would fall and we'd end up tracking crushed, dirty petals into the flat. And I don't want to end up on the bottom of a shoe like that, d'you know what I mean?

'So I got thinking about being a deciduous tree that blooms but doesn't disappear all at once. And then I just ended up picturing the poplars in the Dutch paintings in the Kelvingrove, you know the ones along the canal, with the windmills in the background? That would be perfect, right? All my petals would end up floating on the water when they did eventually fall. A clean, green, blooming machine!'

She didn't mention, or maybe it didn't need to be said, that for as long as we had known each other poplars had always been my favourite.

She talked a while longer about her future tree life: pollinators and birdhouses, and maybe, if she was lucky, even a rope swing, and then we headed back to our flat, on our street, and fell asleep in our bed: wrapped up together like animals asleep beneath the roots of a great tree.

She was always cold so was as usual wearing her fluffy pyjamas while I lay naked alongside her. My hand crept under her top and came to lie on her soft belly. For a moment before we both drifted off I let myself feel her breathing through the gentle rise and fall of her stomach. As I slept I imagined her cracking under my fingers like dry bark.

We were woken that morning by the sun slanting across our faces. I imagined for a moment that I had simply fallen for an elaborate prank, or better yet, that I had dreamt up the entire conversation. Instead, turning round to face me, her eyes still half closed, she said, 'If I'm going to become a tree I'm going to have to start acting like one. I'm off to the park.' I didn't know

175

how to respond. That was the second last thing she ever said to me.

Slowly, slowly she got out of bed and dressed herself in a pair of thick brown corduroys and a bright green top with her heavy black boots on. Sticking out from her hair a single leaf wavered nonchalantly in the air. She looked round once, blew me a kiss, and was out the door.

There are not all that many ways to respond to a goodbye like that, so, not wanting to cause a scene, I waited a while in our bed and stared out the window at the tree whose branches would tap the window on windy nights. Was she having an affair with this tree? Stranger things had happened, in fact they were happening right now. As soon as this thought entered my mind I rushed out after her, walking from park to park across the city.

It was a crisp early spring morning but the farther I went from our flat the more the winds picked up. Before long I was leaning hard into the gale with my coat wrapped tight around me.

Eventually I found her on the hill overlooking the botanics. There she stood, arms in the air, fingers spread wide and already her feet looked to be half in the earth. She seemed to be rustling as she was buffeted by the wind and her joints sighed as she swayed from side to side. She was still a small tree and could have done with one of those plastic cylinders they wrap round spruces, but I could tell that before long she would be tall enough for me to climb her and lie amongst her branches. Or was I to have asked for permission to clamber all over her? I had never asked other trees for permission in the past, but how often was a tree someone's lover? Now that I thought about it I wasn't too sure of that answer either. It struck me then that I would have wanted a little more time to discuss all of this. I suppose I would have quite liked to have done the research with her.

When we first got together we would spend hours researching. It started with UCAS forms, course modules, and exam preparation but before long we were researching accommodation, the history of the city and taking online quizzes to identify what sort of student we would be. However, she always moved so fast that by the time I had got my bearings of a given topic she had exhausted her well of interest and was onto the next discovery. She was always reading herself away into the future while I was barely keeping up with the present.

In the past I sat with her in silence as overhead the clouds tumbled out across the city skyline, and continued sitting there right until the sun had started to disappear in an orange glow. She didn't answer when I asked whether she wanted to come back home so instead I tied a little sign to her arm which read 'TREE IN PROGRESS, DO NOT DISTURB' and headed back to our flat.

That night for the first time in a long time I was cold. I dreamt that she was cut down, chopped up, carved and sanded. I dreamt that she was being sold in IKEA as a flat pack bed frame. I saw my girlfriend and I buying her for our new flat. I remember assembling her in the room we slept in together the night before. I woke up in a bed made from beech, not poplar.

I visited her every night after that. Before long she was taller than me and I couldn't wrap my arms all the way around her middle. She became mossy and I considered giving her face a shave but then conceded it wasn't my place to police her facial hair, much less as a tree. I remembered she had talked about a rope swing so I hung one up over one of her lower branches, making sure that both the rope and the branch were strong enough to support the weight of the little children who played around her trunk. I checked the pH of the soil and pretended I knew what that meant.

I imagined we were really happy together although she never spoke to me. I wondered if she still knew I was there.

We spent a long time like that. Then one day as I lay in her shade someone I had used to know stopped by me as they wandered through the park. A lot had changed since then, he had a new job and my girlfriend had become a tree so it was agreed we would meet that night and catch up about everything that had happened. He headed off and I waited by her trunk one last time. She must have heard what we had discussed but I told her anyway just to be sure. Though I did not mention it directly we both knew what this meant: it would be the first night we had not spent together since she had become a tree.

After sitting a while longer I stood up and got ready to head off into town. Just then, with a big sigh and a great amount of creaking the tree spoke: it sounded like the wind. The wind and the tree said, 'What about me?'

Then came a pause that lasted.

Defusing the Bomb
by Margaret Sessa-Hawkins

Longlisted, Edinburgh Award for Flash Fiction 2023

'Do you know her name yet?' Sonya asks.

In front of them, about two hundred meters away, the bomb sits silent.

'Molly,' Edith says.

Most of the bomb is buried; the hard carapace nestled inside the earth — only a small portion of the fuse is perceptible.

'Molly,' Sonya says, seeming to taste the sound on her tongue. 'I like it.' As she speaks, Sonya uses a remote to carefully maneuver the EOD robot into position.

'I think my family is still nervous about me adopting a teen,' Edith admits. Sonya utters an 'mmmhmmm,' as she begins the delicate work of guiding the EOD's thin metal arm into place to clear the dirt around the bomb's fuse, leaving it open for disposal. Edith watches Sonya, and thinks that to a certain extent, she understands her family's trepidation. She understands the fear of unexploded mines that lurk, just beneath life's surface, waiting for any trigger to set them off.

She knows too though, that the worst does not always happen. Sometimes the bomb squad arrives in time.

'Well,' Sonya says, the robot's arm retracting after it brushes away the last of the dirt. 'They'll come around once Molly is here.' She pushes a button, and the EOD fires a quick jet of water into the fuse. There is a small pop, a tiny puff of smoke.

'I know they will,' Edith affirms. In front of them, all is still.

Sometimes, everything works out. Sometimes, you defuse the bomb.

June to September
by Sam Oakley

Longlisted, Edinburgh Award for Flash Fiction 2023

I was born on 15th June; my daughter arrives on 22nd. There are forty years between us. I was tugged into the world by forceps, following a battle. My daughter swims into warm waters, scooped up for her first greedy breath in my arms. She is perfection. Days and nights merge, feeding her, gazing at her, breathing the warm biscuit smell of that fuzzy dark head.

My mother held me on 2nd July; it would be 28 years before she would do so again. Was I snatched from her arms or did she pass me away? Somehow, she left. Home to the family who'd concealed her disgrace. My daughter receives visits like royalty: grandparents, aunts and uncles, friends and neighbours. They bring presents and cards, laughter and cake.

On 3rd July I was transacted to temporary 'care'. At the back of my wardrobe I keep a paper bag with pitiful oddments of clothing and a doll sewn from scraps. It's so misshapen I can't bear to look at it. My daughter lies with her bunny, her Lizzie and her bear.

On 12th September a car pulled up and a couple emerged. They were smartly dressed. There was cooing and pleasantries. The paperwork had been completed. It recorded that I was small and slow, but I could go 'home'. My birth could be falsified; my name could change.

On 12th September I hold my daughter so tight I fear I will never let her go.

Into the Green
by Kat Nicholls

Longlisted, Edinburgh Award for Flash Fiction 2023

The mill had sent my crew deep into the back woods, surveying old growth timber. Bosses said they'd make the Feds see sense after the logging was done. Money usually works.

The newbie didn't like it, kept sayin' this was protected land. Given a choice I wouldn'ta brought her. I had to warn Hank off her three times.

We were headin' back when it happened. First sign we had was Joe disappearing. We never saw him vanish. We searched but that just split us up.

Then the screamin' started. I think it was screaming. I've never heard any sound like that in my whole life. It scared me like nothing ever has. I just lit outta there like hell itself was after me. I looked back once. That's when I saw Hank. He's standin' there and, damned if his body isn't changin', stretching up like it's pulled taffy. He starts sprouting leaves, skin starts growing bark. 'Fore I knew it there was this huge tree right where he'd been.

That's when I saw her. The newbie. Only she's different. Call me crazy but there's bark on her skin and her fingers? They're too long, too many bends an' joints to 'em. She smiled at me then patted Hank's tree.

She let me go. Why? Maybe to carry this message to you suits. Stay outta those woods! You wanna to know why all your teams have disappeared? That's why. She said it was protected land. She meant it.

The Promise of Wildflowers
by Lisa Fransson

Longlisted, Edinburgh Award for Flash Fiction 2023

Two hares streak out of the wood and onto the meadow behind the Stephenson's house. First the female, then the mad-for-her March male. Mrs Stephenson watches them through her bedroom window, clutches her cardigan tight against the dawn chill as the female turns and starts throwing punches something fierce. How those hares bounce around. In a few weeks, this meadow will be a sea of buttercups, cow parsley, harebells. But for now, the female is standing her ground in the tall grass.

Behind her a snore catches in Mr Stephenson's throat. He coughs and opens his eyes, swings his legs to the floor, oozes sweat concentrated enough to strip paint with.

Mrs Stephenson glances out the window, where the male is chasing the female again, around and around the meadow, but suddenly the female turns, throws herself at the male, jabbing, jabbing, jabbing. He cowers, recedes, and takes flight back into the woods.

The she-hare sits down in the tall grass, looks around her, nibbles at one stalk of grass, then another, as if the world was hers, and hers alone.

'Look at the state of you, clumsy bitch,' rasps Mr Stephenson.

Mrs Stephenson touches the swelling on her cheek, then, with the sun rising behind, her, she turns and pulls back her fist.

The Parting Glass
by T.L. Ransome

Longlisted, Edinburgh Award for Flash Fiction 2023

Tar was melting on the roads. The grass was dead, the skeeters scorched, the lizards cooking in the shade.

Jhune's truck was parked at Long Lake and she'd been mobbed for two hours. Most ice cream truck drivers looked like shifty ex-cons so twinkle-eyed Jhune had always been popular with moms.

Jhune looked out at her regulars and sighed. This was her last day. She'd started 27 years ago with a cooler full of Dixie cups. It was her summer break from teaching brilliant but nefarious third graders.

'Miss Jhune!' Maria walked over.

'Hi! How're y'all?'

'Oh, fine. Three Drumsticks, please. So…,' Maria leaned in, '…did y'all hear?'

'What?'

'About the robbery at Eldorado Jewelry this morning.'

'Yeah. I heard the sirens. That's awful.'

'I know. I-'

There was a scream. Maria's seven-year-old was being attacked by a duck.

Jhune chuckled and left. She drove slowly past the park and the supermarket, saying goodbye to her town.

She'd become an expert at saying goodbye. She said goodbye to a class of students every May. She said goodbye to her four children as they left the nest. She said goodbye to her husband who'd had a heart attack in December.

This time, she'd be the one leaving.

She rumbled into the airport parking lot and said goodbye to her truck.

On the plane, a stewardess asked, 'White wine, ma'am? Ice water?'

'Wine, thanks,' Jhune said. She'd brought all the ice she needed. And this ice wouldn't melt, even in Cabo.

Star Eaters
by Iona Rule

Longlisted, Edinburgh Award for Flash Fiction 2023

When the stars started disappearing we thought light pollution was obscuring them but astronomers confirmed their absence. They didn't know why.

Nobody considered the wishes. Stars could grant wishes — not world peace, they were too small, but little wishes like 'Please let the cute girl on the bus say yes.' Wishes floated skywards to catch on the flypaper stars. As stars disappeared, they gathered like lint, ignored and unfulfilled.

One night I made a wish on the head of Ursa Major when it vanished. A net had appeared and snatched it out of the sky. The light was bundled into an ice cream van and driven away. No one believed me.

Later I learned the truth. The stars had been sold to be crushed and then licked off silver spoons. They would fizz in their bellies and make their eyes shine.

By then all the stars had been harvested and the world looked up at a blank vastness. The elite, all sparkle-eyed, commissioned new stars. They shot diamantés to the heavens on paper planes and astronauts draped fairy lights across the heavens on pegs. Each star was sponsored. Elon Musk had a whole constellation. The head of Ursa Major was returned but if you looked closely you could see golden arches on its surface.

The wishes couldn't latch onto these baubles though. Even if they could, what use were wishes on plastic? I hoped some wishes kept going, gliding through the dark. Searching for a star that wasn't yet dead.

Do not open anything until it is paid for
by Sally Curtis

Longlisted, Edinburgh Award for Flash Fiction 2023

I am used to clamour and clatter, jostle and jangle. Voices calling, tempting, soaring above each other, their jumble of words wheeling into the dazzling cerulean sky, up and up, past the clouds.

'What do you want lady? You want this? You want these? I have the freshest. The best.'

Colour piled rainbow-high, skin upon skin, pressed close, one thousand aromas assailing my senses, one thousand tastes tantalizing my tongue. Yellow and green and purple and orange toppled together; salty and spicy buffered against sweet and sour; some whisper warmly, others shout, hot and zesty. Skins soft, skins hard, skins pitted, skins smooth.

I am not used to these neatly ordered rows, this organisation:

type,

size,

brand,

price.

What is imprisoned in these identical cans? What is confined in these jars and packets? What hides behind the paper labels?

Cus-tard?

Mar-ma-lade?

Peas without pods?

Vegetables, their roots washed clean?

Amongst the squared bread suffocating in plastic custody, a lone mango nestles, separated from its kind. Something else in the wrong place.

I take it in my hands, feeling the scent of home, cradling the colour of belonging. Its skin is bruised and dented, the flesh probably browned, but it too has survived an unwilling journey to find refuge amongst the unknown.

I lift it to my lips, brush its tender skin and whisper, 'You are safe now.'

Opportunity
by Tilly Lavenás

Longlisted, Edinburgh Award for Flash Fiction 2023

'Is that a Bouvier des Flandres?' Alice asked the elderly woman with the large black dog.

'Yes!' Edwina was surprised. People who could identify Bailey's breed were rare.

'My last dog was a Bouvier,' Alice said. 'It was the saddest day of my life when Pierre had to be put down.'

Edwina made a suitably sad face.

'They're so dignified,' Alice pressed on, 'and warm to strangers. I used to say Pierre could be salesman of the year!'

She had won a friend. Only two days later, she encountered Edwina again, they talked about Bouvier rescue organisations and Crufts. Soon they were going together to dog shows and out for meals. Alice learned much about Edwina. Edwina showed less curiosity about her new and younger friend.

Then Edwina caught Covid.

Alice did her shopping, ran errands, walked Bailey.

Edwina lasted a few months. In her will, she left Alice £10,000.

This was not unexpected, though Alice thought it could have been more. Edwina hadn't mentioned the nephew in Singapore.

One milky morning in a large park across town, Alice met a white-haired man who moved slowly, with a stick in one hand and a dog's lead in the other. He looked like someone who had time to fill in.

'Is that a Bedlington Terrier?'

He nodded, pleased.

'My last dog was a Bedlington,' said Alice. 'They're such genuine dogs, aren't they? When Dylan died, it was the saddest day of my life!'

How to Eat a Mango
by Jennifer Jones

Longlisted, Edinburgh Award for Flash Fiction 2023

You must wait for the golden blush that says, 'I'm ready.' Then gently cup it in your hands and hold it to your nose. Breathe in. If its fragrance is sweet and freely given, the time has come to devour it.

Using a fine sharp blade, slice the plump flesh from its possessive seed. Then carve the liberated fruit into bite size cubes, careful not to pierce the skin that cradles it.

Note the glistening richness of its juicy offering then raise it to your lips. By instinct, the tongue won't wait. It will reach out to savour the luscious softness, beating the lips by a full second. The teeth will eagerly follow, tearing a cube of flesh from its protective skin. One by glorious one, bitesize chunks of ecstasy will tumble around your mouth until you are forced to let them go and swallow.

Your body may quiver with delight. The tendency to groan is common. Many cast aside good manners to lick, not just the plate but fingers and forearms as well. To avoid embarrassment, it is best to perform this ritual alone or with a loved one. A fresh, ripe mango is a gift from the gods. Time stands still when absorbed in its sticky succulence. Surrender to it, for in that moment, nothing else matters until it's gone and you find yourself longing for another.

The mango itself might not last but the memory of your first will never leave you.

The Scottish Arts Trust Story Awards

scottishartstrust.org

The Scottish Arts Trust, established in 2014, supports the arts through voluntary action. The Trust provides platforms for showcasing the work of artists, writers, musicians and other arts practitioners, while also mobilising and drawing on the skills, energy and vision of volunteers committed to the creative arts.

Initiatives include awards, exhibitions, performances and publications in the visual and literary arts as well as contemporary music and the promotion of young musicions. The Trust aims to expand these opportunities by building on the experience of volunteers who seek a closer involvement with the arts. Currently, more than fifty volunteers are involved in the operation of our projects.

From the outset, the Trust has benefitted from the support of the Scottish Arts Club in Edinburgh, Scotland. The Club was founded in 1873 by a group of artists and sculptors, including Sir John Steell, Sculptor to Queen Victoria, and Sir George Harvey, President of the Royal Scottish Academy. For twenty years they met in a series of premises around the West End of Edinburgh. In 1894, the building at 24 Rutland Square was purchased as a meeting place for men involved and interested in all arts disciplines. It was not until 1982, following contentious debate, that women were admitted as club members. In 1998, Mollie Marcellino became its first female President. Until her death in 2018, Mollie was also an avid reader for the short story competition.

The idea for the short story competition, which is open to writers worldwide, developed out of the Scottish Arts Club Writers Group. Alexander McCall Smith has long been a supporter and honorary member of the Scottish Arts Club, which has sometimes featured in his Scotland Street novels. He volunteered to be chief judge and remained in that role until 2020 when Andrew O'Hagan took over, followed by another long-standing honorary member of the club, Ian Rankin, in 2022.

Our chief judges are aided by a team of readers whose primary qualifications are a love of short fiction and a willingness to read, debate, defend and promote their favourites through successive rounds of the competition — a process that takes four or five months. In 2022, we established a Readers Register for volunteers around the world who would like to serve as readers for the writing awards.

Short story prize money has increased from a first prize of £300 in 2014 to £1,000 by 2017 and £3,000 in 2023. In 2017 we launched the Isobel Lodge Award, named after a dear member of the Scottish Arts Club Writers Group. This prize, which rose to £750 in 2020 is given to the top story entered in the competition by an unpublished writer born, living or studying in Scotland.

In 2018 we introduced the Edinburgh Award for Flash Fiction, with novelist Sandra Ireland as the chief judge. Sandra won the first of our short story competitions with her story, *The Desperation Game*, which lent its title to our first anthology. In 2021, celebrated authors Zoë Strachan and Louise Welsh took over as the flash fiction judges. In 2023, the flash fiction prize rose to £2,000 and the Golden Hare Award for the top flash fiction entry from Scotland to £500.

The Write Mango Awards, for stories that are 'fun, amusing, bizarre and as delicious as a mango' were introduced in 2023 to encourage more writers to submit entertaining laugh-out-loud or quirky tales.

We enjoy celebrating the work of our short story finalists at the annual Story Awards Dinner held at the Scottish Arts Club — and the flash fiction writers at the highly entertaining Flash Bash.

The Scottish Arts Trust is a registered charity. All funds raised through our competitions are used to promote the arts in Scotland. Learn more about the programmes supported by the Scottish Arts Trust at scottishartstrust.org.

Acknowledgements

Our thanks to international best-selling author, Ian Rankin, who took over as chief judge of the short story award in 2022 and to award-winning authors Zoë Strachan and Louise Welsh who continued as chief judges of the flash fiction award.

We are grateful to John Lodge whose donations support the Isobel Lodge Award, which brings such encouragement to many unpublished short story writers in Scotland. Thanks also to Sir Mark Jones whose support for the Golden Hare Award has helped to promote interest in the flash format across Scotland.

Our teams of dedicated readers reviewed and discussed over 1,500 entries to the short and flash fiction competitions in 2022. We are in awe of the energy and commitment the readers bring to successive rounds of these competitions and their passion as they make the case for the stories they love to progress through the competition.

We are indebted to Dai Lowe who works tirelessly as our story awards administrator, to Siobhán Coward who manages the short story readers and to Linda Grieg who does the same for the flash fiction teams. Our thanks also to Gordon Mitchell whose wonderful paintings give the story awards and our anthologies such a distinctive visual style. We are grateful to Amy Macrae for inspiring revisions to the story awards brand. On a personal level, I am thankful for the cheerful, meticulous and skilled professionalism of my co-editor, Claire Rocha.

Finally, a huge thank you to all the writers who have imagined, drafted, written, re-written and submitted stories in 2022. Your stories are packed with inspiration and creative passion. We look forward to reading more!

Sara Cameron McBean
Director, Scottish Arts Trust Story Awards
scottishartstrust.org

Printed in Great Britain
by Amazon

37192485R00111